A HIGHLAND ꓘ FOR HANNAH

MYSTIC FALLS
BOOK ONE

MARY WARREN

To anyone who has ever felt unworthy of their dreams, you are worthy. No matter your size, you are worthy of your dreams.

DEAR READER,

This book is a long time in the making. I have been writing novels my whole life, but I have never finished one, until now. I know that has a lot to do with the Fat Girls in Fiction community and all the healing I have found in reading and sharing fat representation with the world. Between these pages you will find laughter and tears, a little bit of magic and a whole lot of heart. I hope you also find a sense of healing, knowing there is someone out there for you regardless of you size. You are worthy of your dreams.

Content Warning - Graphic sexual content, Minor injury, Failing health of a parent, Supporting character dealing with internal fat phobia.

CHAPTER 1

"*A*re you listening to me, Hannah?" Roger Glass asked. "I am going to need you to put a little more effort in."

Maybe it was the way her boss disregarded her hours of work. Maybe it was the all-nighter she had just pulled. Maybe it was the text from her boyfriend right before the meeting saying he couldn't make it to her family's stupid field day tradition. Whatever it was, something inside her shifted.

She had been working her ass off for the firm. She had the most billable hours, the best record, and was continually overlooked for promotions. When the men around her climbed the ladder faster, she took it in stride. She was used to the misogyny growing up in certain culture. But when Brittney Williams was promoted after winning a case that Hannah had done most of the work for, she realized it wasn't about being a woman.

It was about her appearance. Hannah had never really fit into society's beauty standards. She was fat—she had been her entire life. She had accepted it but knew people made assumptions about her because of it. She also knew it made certain parts of her life harder. So, she worked harder and let people treat her in unacceptable ways. It was exhausting. Anticipating needs and compensating for a perceived fault. She had given up trying to change her body for the world. But her mental health was still in tatters blazing that trail in her career. A career she had come to realize a little too late that wasn't her passion.

But that ended that day. Hannah Glenn was done.

"With all due respect, Mr. Glass, I have been putting in an immense effort. I have shown my value time and time again, but it is never recognized," she said, calm.

Showing emotion would lead to her being completely written off as a hysterical woman. She knew the culture all too well.

"I see your work, but this firm has a public image. That image is important."

"And you don't think I fit the public image of Glass & Associates?"

"Hannah, I need you to get back to work," he said with a dismissing flick of his hand.

"I am good at what I do, so why is everyone around me getting promoted, while I am stuck?"

"Hannah, we are done here." He straightened the stack of papers without a glance at her.

Hannah thought for a minute about all the late nights, about all the long hours, about all the errands she ran, while still doing most of the work with no recognition.

"Yeah . . . ya know what . . . we are done here, or at least I am," she said before standing, as if the words coming out of her mouth surprised her.

"What is it exactly you are saying, Ms. Glenn?, and I would be very careful here." He eyed her, clearly losing his patience.

"I quit."

"No, you don't, get back to work."

"Sir, I do. I quit. I could take it when the men around me moved up the ladder. I get it. It's a man's game. But when you promoted Brittney with the work I did and the hours I spent researching and talking to clients, I obviously do not fit the 'image' you speak of."

"I'm not sure what you're referring to."

"I am referring to the fact that you do not want to promote me because of the way I look. I am done, sir. I don't even like this job. We are not nice people. I'm not even sure why I'm here. I quit."

"Hannah—"

Hannah turned and walked to the door. She looked back at the sputtering man one last time, who was fuming in front of a backdrop of the city from his office window. The look on his face was seething with shock.

"Hannah, if you walk out that door you are fired. You won't work in this city again."

"You can't fire me. I already quit." She turned on her heel and walked out as the door closed behind her.

That felt good. That felt REALLY good, she thought.

Adrenaline coursed through her body as she strolled to her desk. All eyes were on her. She didn't even care; she had only become a lawyer because it was what her father had wanted, and she was good at it. She didn't need that. After grabbing her purse, she walked to the elevator, feeling a million pounds lighter.

She couldn't believe she had just quit her job; it was not a part of her five-year plan. Hannah didn't normally operate that way. She anticipated the crushing anxiety of being jobless . . . but it wasn't coming anytime soon. She had saved enough money to be okay for a while. Relief. That was all she felt.

She made her way home to her walk-up in Brooklyn on a high. City life had never suited her much, with being a homebody. And if she was honest, she had always felt most at home at her family's farmhouse upstate, where she was headed. She was going to pack up, head there for a few weeks, and figure out her next step. She would spend a couple of weeks riding horses, talking to her best friend, and gaining some perspective.

As she turned the key to her apartment, the dulcet tones of her boyfriend yelling over his gaming headset greeted her. Her boyfriend had just texted her, backing out of a family obligation because he had to work. Her boyfriend, who she had just lent $450 to for rent—not rent they shared because, although he had asked multiple times, he did not live with her.

"What are you doing here?" she asked. "Why aren't you at work?"

He looked at her like his mother had just caught him playing hooky. He was in a stained hoodie, and his hair looked a couple of days past a wash.

"Hey, bro. I gotta go," he said as he pulled the headset off. "Babe, what are you doing home early?"

"I quit my job today." She waited for the panic, but it didn't come. "What are you doing here, in my apartment? Why aren't you at work or at least your OWN apartment?"

"I didn't think you'd be here."

"Clearly." Hannah stared at him, waiting for an excuse.

"I quit my job three weeks ago. I just can't do schedules like that."

"Schedules like what? You worked at a deli."

"Yeah, they wanted me there at like seven every morning. That is not how I thrive, babe. You know me. I just can't—"

"Okay, whatever, but why are you here?"

"Carlos's girlfriend moved in with us, and she is always

on my case. Makes it seem like the house needs to be quiet, like a fucking library or something. I had to tiptoe all day, so I just come here when you go to work."

Rage gripped Hannah. In the past, she may have let it slide, but something shifted that day.

"Excuse me! She's a nurse, who works the third shift, so you should respect her sleep. And you come here often?"

"Just since I quit the deli. It's not a big deal. I basically live here, anyway." He stood from the couch, walked over to Hannah, and put his hands on her shoulders.

"It IS a big deal. If I wanted you to live here, I would have said yes the times you brought it up." She brushed his hands away and looked at him.

"Calm down, babe. It's just so much nicer here. It's fine."

That did it. She was not going to calm down.

"And correct me if I'm wrong, but didn't you just back out of game day with my family because you have to work?"

"I didn't wanna go . . . You don't wanna go. Why don't we both just stay here?"

"Andy . . . I have to go. It's my family."

"So, what, you have to go, so I have to go?"

"Ummm . . . yeah, that is how this whole relationship thing works."

Hannah took a deep breath. With having just shaken the corporate world, she considered maybe it was time at home, too. All she got out of the relationship was mediocre sex, after having had put up with his crap for over a year. It wasn't necessarily that he had never paid or that he had never remembered her birthday. It was that he felt like a chore, like one more task on a checklist. That is not how relationships should be. She deserved better. She deserved better at work and at home. She had already blown her life up once that day, so she might as well have blown it up all the way. Hannah was never one to half-ass anything.

"Ya know what. I'm on a roll today. We're done."

"What?" he said, looking at her, slack-jawed.

"Yeah, we are done. I deserve better."

"Babe, come on, let's talk about this." He reached for her again, but she blocked his advance.

"No, let's not. Get your stuff together and go home."

"Come on, I'll go and let you calm down." He turned away from her and grabbed his phone and keys before mumbling, "Plus, no one else is knocking down your door."

"I'm sorry. What did you just say to me?"

"Babe."

"No, I am a smart, capable woman. I've been putting up with too much for too long. I am done. We are done. This is not who I am. Get your stuff and get out."

"Fine, but don't come crawling back when—"

"Oh, I won't. You can count on that. Give me your key."

He went over to the TV, unplugged his Xbox, and walked over to Hannah, who had her hand open, waiting for the key.

"You're such a bitch sometimes." He took the key off his chain, put it in her hand, and stormed out the door.

"Thank you for making this easy," she called as she slammed the door behind him.

She was fuming. In the span of two hours, she had blown up her life. She had quit a job where she was not appreciated. She had broken up with her slacker boyfriend, who was stuck in his college days, with no sign of growth. She was done dealing with it. Nothing was going to change until she took a stand. She reached for her purse and rummaged around for her phone.

Hannah: I'm coming into town tomorrow. Drinks?

Poppy: You know it. I'm off at 5.

With that, Hannah Glenn poured herself a glass of wine and packed. She didn't know what her plan was yet, but she knew some changes were about to come her way.

CHAPTER 2

*H*annah and Poppy had been best friends since the third grade, when Hannah spent most of her summers at her family's farmhouse. Poppy's family ran the apple orchard neighboring the farm.

Poppy's brother, Sam, had been stabling their horses since the last stable hand retired earlier that month. Hannah knew he didn't mind and welcomed the extra money; she also knew he was in the middle of the busy season at their orchard, so he needed his time back. Hannah would be happy to take care of the horses, since she was staying there.

Taking a horse out for long ride was a good way to clear your head. While there, figuring her own shit out, she would add "find a new groom" to that list. The list expanded, but Hannah reminded herself she was strong and capable and that, if anyone could get their life back on track, it was her. She just needed a pros and cons list. Yes, she would add "make a list" to her list.

The previous night, while imbibing copious amounts of wine, Poppy had informed Hannah they would be going to the renaissance fair in town, offering Hannah an outfit she nearly spilled out of.

"Poppy, I can't wear this. One false move, and these are gonna fall right out," Hannah protested, looking at her barely contained bosom.

"I say, if you got 'em, flaunt 'em, and you definitely got 'em," Poppy said.

Of course Poppy had multiple ren faire outfits. Poppy was a free spirit, something Hannah had loved about her, although a foreign one to that of Hannah's.

After parking at the county fairgrounds, they stepped out of the car to adjust themselves. Hannah wore a peasant shirt with a long purple skirt and a green corset with gold details. She shoved her boobs back into the corset, and her long, wavy blonde hair fell over her shoulders. She caught a glimpse of herself in the car window, turning her head with a shrug of approval. Poppy wore a red dress with a black corset, her sleek dark hair braided down her back with red poppies woven in. She and Hannah had a similar body shape, so they shared clothes, but that was about where the similarities ended.

"Shall we?" Poppy said with a smile.

Arm in arm, they walked to the front gate.

They spent the afternoon walking around, taking in the sights. They watched fine men in kilts sing some sea shanties, cheered on some brave knights at a joust, drank cider, and shared a funnel cake. All in all, it had been a wonderful day at the ren faire.

They stopped to rest on a bench to watch a puppet show.

"So, what's your plan? I know you; you took your day, and now, you have a plan," Poppy said before licking powdered sugar off her finger.

"Ya know, I feel like I should. I always have, but I don't."

"Seriously?" Poppy looked at her with raised eyebrows.

"Yeah, I am. I have always done what I am supposed to do. School, college, law school, climbing the ladder at a major firm, but I don't think any of it is what I actually wanted."

Hannah had never uttered those words to anyone. Her family had this pristine image to uphold, one she felt like she did not fit in, and Hannah had overcompensated by working hard and holding herself to ridiculously high standards. Only since exploring the idea had she realized it no longer served her.

"If you could do anything, what would you do?" Poppy asked.

"If I am being honest, I would live at the farmhouse, marry an amazing guy, have endless amazing sex, write romance novels, and live my best life. But we all know the family I'm from and the expectations that go with it. And I'm a damn good lawyer."

Ever since high school, when Hannah stumbled upon the romance novels on her mother's bookshelves, Hannah loved them. She loved to get swept away in a story. The men in the books shared their feelings and took care of the women they loved. Hannah wished she could find real men like that, but she was starting to think they didn't exist.

So, Hannah did what she was supposed to: became a self-sufficient lawyer. She could count on herself, and everyone else counted on her, too.

"Screw being a good lawyer and screw expectations. You did that. I think it is time you did what makes you happy. I have read some of your stories. They're good. I say do it. Find yourself a hunky guy and write romance novels," Poppy encouraged.

"Okay . . . poof! Hunky guys. Poof! A publishing deal."

"I'm glad we're on the same page." Poppy hooked her arm through Hannah's, and they went on to enjoy the fair.

They came to a sign that read "Bridget's Love Spells and Fortune Telling."

"Ooooo, let's go in! We need to get you a love spell for your hunky sex god so you can start livin' the dream, baby," Poppy joked.

Hannah laughed at her, but in they went.

"Oh, hello. Welcome, my dears. How can I help ye today?" asked a short round woman who had wild red hair with some gray around the temples. The women's eyes twinkled with magic, and she had a thick Scottish brogue.

"Yes. We need a love spell," Poppy said with a big grin.

Hannah elbowed her.

"What? You do. You need a sexy guy to live out your romance novel dreams with. Didn't you just tell me that?"

"Are ye searching for love, lass? Well, you've come to the right place," the woman said to Hannah with a knowing smile.

"I mean . . . maybe."

"Tell me about him," said the woman.

Hannah felt silly, but she couldn't stop herself. She talked about what she wanted in a partner, as if the words flowed out of her on their own.

"I want a man I don't have to take care of. A man who can solve his own problems and live his own life but join me in mine. A man whom I can count on to be there when I need him. A man that helps me shoulder the burdens of life. I want romance. I want butterflies when I hear him laugh. I want to feel that spark when he kiss me. I want a someone who finds my body, how it is right now, attractive and doesn't want me to lose weight or dress a certain way, and I want to be unbearably attracted to him. I want him to make me laugh and make me feel alive. And of course, we must have mind-blowing sex, like all the orgasms."

Poppy looked at Hannah, her mouth agape.

The woman had been tinkering with herbs and oils.

"So, ya know . . . . that should be totally doable," she joked, knowing the man of her dreams could never exist.

"You are in luck, my dear. Tonight is the equinox. When the moon is high in the sky, light a fire and follow these steps." She placed a bag of herbs and a scroll of paper in Hannah's hand.

"Okay, thank you. How much do I owe you?"

"Love spells are twenty dollars," she said, pointing to her sign.

"Twenty dollars!" Hannah said. "That seems a little high for a bag of dry herbs."

"Trust me," she said with a wink. "This will be worth every penny."

Hannah sighed, took out her wallet, and paid, then they turned to leave.

"Thank you," Poppy called back to the woman.

"It was my pleasure, lassies. Enjoy the fair," she called as the two of them stepped out to the main thoroughfare.

"So, are you going to do the spell tonight?" Poppy asked, barely containing excitement.

"No."

"Why not?" she pleaded. "I think it'll be good for you. Sometimes, participating in rituals like that can help you to figure out what you want. I'm not saying some handsome rogue in a kilt will appear. I'm just saying maybe you will figure some stuff out, ya know?"

Hannah thought about it, and maybe Poppy was right. Something about performing rituals made you think about what you truly wanted, and right then, her mind was cloudy. What she wanted seemed so silly. She had a law degree and a great apartment in Brooklyn—why would she give all that up? What would her family say?

And honestly, she would have to tell them that the next

weekend was the Glenn family game weekend, one of Hannah's least favorite weekends of the entire year. Her whole picture-perfect family would get together and compete in physical games. Her immediate family, plus her aunt and uncle and cousins, would descend on the farm that weekend. It served as a reunion and a way to remind Hannah how different she was from her family. This time, she would have no job and no boyfriend. That thought set a boulder in her stomach. She was going to do it, anything for a little clarity.

That night, Hannah made her way down to the fire pit. The wind blew the chilly autumn air, and she hugged her hoodie. Earlier in the evening, she had got the wood ready, so all she had to do was light the match. The fire's glow warmed her. She looked up at the clear night sky. The moon was high in the sky, just like that woman had said. She was preparing for the spell.

She felt silly, but she pushed through. She needed to figure out what her next step should be. She was tired of working a job that killed her joy, tired of accepting treatment she didn't deserve. She knew her worth. But knowing your worth and demanding it from others were not the same thing, and she was not very good at that last part. It was time. She needed to do it, or she would end up back in the city with a job at a new firm, dating men who required more parenting than partnering.

The autumn air's chill disappeared as Hannah sat by the fire examining the spell. She opened the bag, read the instructions on the paper, and got to work. She placed the little crystals in a circle around the fire, sprinkled salt on the fire, and watched the flames shift colors. She took the bundle of dried herbs, threw them on the fire, and read the incantation aloud.

· · ·

AIR an oidhche o thoir mo ghaol thugman.
Thar ùine agus àite leig leis tighinn thugman.

SHE HOPED she had said that right, recognizing it as Gaelic but didn't know how to say any of the words.

She watched the fire; the flames had returned to their usual orange glow, and her mind stirred in wonder. She thought about what she and Poppy had talked about and what she had told the woman at the ren faire. What she really wanted was a slower life. A life where she was the writer she had always dreamed of being. A life where she had a partner to support her and her work. A partner who cared for her in the same way she cared for him—and, of course, someone with whom she had mind-blowing sex. Why did this seem so simple but like such a pipe dream at the same time? She watched the fire burn under the moon of the autumn equinox and dreamed about what life could be.

CHAPTER 3

*H*annah woke up the next morning with the sun. She was tired from her late night, but she headed out to take care of the horses who needed to be fed and be put in the pasture for the day. The coffee machine grumbled to life, and she slipped on some shoes. She wore her oversized law school hoodie and a pair of tie-dye leggings, her hair pulled up in a messy bun on top of her head. She made her way through the dewy grass down to the stable that housed her family's horses.

She opened the big barn door to the horse's soft whinny.

"Good morning, girl," Hannah said, flipping a switch, kicking on the light's soft hum.

"Aye!" a strange male voice called from up in the hayloft.

Startled, she called out, "Who's there?"

She looked at the man towering above her in the hayloft, who wore a kilt, looking totally out of place.

"Who are you? Did Sam send you? Why are you wearing that?"

"Look, lassie, I dinna ken where I am. I dinna ken who

Sam is, and as to what I am wearing, I might ask ye the same question. I've never seen a lassie wear such."

Hannah's mind reeled.

"Well, you're on my family's farm, so I'm the one who is asking questions. Who are you, and why are you here?" Fear and anger coursed through her body.

"Lassie, I mean ye no harm. I'm Graham MacNeil. I'm not certain where I am or how I came to be here."

"You need to leave," Hannah said, trying to push back the fear.

"Aye, but first, could you tell me where I am?"

"You are at my family's farm in upstate New York."

"York?" Bewilderment fell across his face.

"New York . . . upstate."

"I'm sorry, I'm not following." He pinched his eyebrows together.

"New York state. In America."

"America?" Shock swept his features. "As in, the colonies."

"Uhhhh . . . . what? Are you on drugs?"

Because that was the only explanation for any of that.

"How did I come to be here?" he asked.

Hannah shook her head in disbelief, thoughts still racing. Graham climbed down the ladder and made his way over to Hannah in three long strides.

"How am I supposed to know that? You're the one in my parents' hayloft. I know how I came to be here."

"This canna be . . ." His eyes were big, stunned.

Things were starting to make sense to Hannah . . . but it was not possible . . . was it? No, it was not possible.

"Should I call someone? Should I take you to a hospital?"

"Call someone? . . . Hospital? I'm afraid I dinna ken the way of the Americas, and I dinna ken how I came to be here."

"Ummmm, what year do you think it is?" Hannah asked tentatively, hoping she was wrong.

"I reckon it is 1745."

"Shut the fuck up!" Hannah gasped.

"What is it?" he asked, looking like he was trying to read Hannah's utter shock.

"That is not possible. This is not possible. This is a dream. I'm going back to bed." Hannah turned and headed out of the barn.

Footsteps followed her.

She turned and yelled, "Do not come near me!"

He put his hands up. "Like I said, lass, I mean ye no harm. I have already tried to wake from this dream, but I dinna think it is a dream."

Hannah looked at him, shaking her head. "This is not possible."

"I agree with ye. Except, here I am, and here ye are, and I know I am flesh and bone, and ye seem to be flesh and bone yerself." He looked at the small tractor in the stall next to him, then looked at the overhead light and said, "Ye asked me what year it was. Now I am going to ask ye the same."

"It is 2020."

His mouth fell open, and his body slackened for a moment before whispering, "That is not possible."

"That's what I said!"

"But somehow, here we are, and I dinna think it is a dream." He looked around, whispering, "Perhaps I was carried here by the fairie folk."

"By who?"

"The fairie folk."

"The fairie folk?"

"Aye, the fairie folk," he said, irritation seeping into his words.

What Hannah had been thinking during the encounter came crashing to the foreground.

"Oh my god . . ." Hannah said, feeling as if all the breath

left her body. She sat on the dewy grass, trying to wrap her head around what she knew in her bones to be true.

"What is it, lass? Are ye hurt?" The great Scotsman went to her on the grass. He knelt next to her, reaching out a tentative hand, then pulled it back.

She didn't speak right away. How could she? How could this be true? Did the spell bring this ancient Scotsman from over two hundred years prior? Just that thought made her feel absolutely insane, yet she somehow knew it to be true.

"Speak, lass, how can I help ye?" Graham looked at her, his eyes tight with concern.

She looked at him, and for the first time, she took him in. He was a tall man, probably well over six feet, with wavy red hair that fell to his shoulders tied into a low ponytail, broad solid shoulders, a kilt of green and blue plaid with a thin yellow streak, and green eyes full of kindness and passion.

Crouched next to her, he examined her with a concerned gaze.

She hyperventilated, her heart racing. She was about to have a full-blown panic attack. Though she had never had one, this had to be what it felt like. Then, all at once, her vision blurred, bringing on her dizziness. Surrounding lights faded to black.

When she came to her senses, she heard birds chirping, and she felt a cool hand brush across her cheek. She opened her eyes; the towering Scotsman had been kneeling over her. She pushed him away and sat up, her head still spinning. She slowly came to, hoping to wake from one of her weirdest dreams, but there he was. No such luck.

"Aye, take it easy, lass. Ye fainted," he said in an almost indistinguishable Scottish brogue.

"You're here. It wasn't a dream," she mused, looking at his face and noting the concern in his eyes.

"Aye, I'm still here. Are ye feeling well, lass?"

She tried to stand. She took his hand, and he helped her up.

"Wait here, and I'll go get yer father," he said as he steadied her on her feet.

"My father is not here."

"Brother?"

Hannah shook her head.

"Uncle, grandsire . . . guardian?"

"I'm here by myself," said Hannah.

"A woman . . . here by herself?" he said, as if he could hardly believe it.

"Yes, I'm a woman, and I'm here by myself," she retorted, her voice sharp with irritation.

"Look at this place. I scarce think a woman of yer upbringing should be left alone and dressed in such a way."

Hannah bristled at his assumption about her inability to take care of herself.

"Woah, excuse me! I can take care of myself, and I don't need a man. Plus, these are fine clothes for feeding horses in." She looked down at her leggings and hoodie. "You are in my time, buddy. I am just fine."

He looked offended, yet impressed.

"Fiery one, I like that. Do ye ken how I came to be in yer time?"

"Ummmm . . . well . . ." she said.

How could she possibly explain what had happened?

His gaze turned suspicious.

"I might know . . . maybe, though it seems highly unlikely. Well . . . my best guess at this moment in time is that . . . ." Struggling, she grappled with how to explain.

"Spit it out, will ye?" he barked.

"I went to a ren faire yesterday with my best friend. We bought a spell from a woman. I did it last night, thinking it would not work and maybe it would just help me make up my mind. But I'm thinking now that, maybe somehow, it was actual magic, as crazy as that sounds. And now, you are here, and . . . and I know I don't know what to do, but that is nonsense. It makes no sense. None of that stuff is real. I believe in science, not magic. Science. I'm team Bill Nye the Science Guy all the way." Words spewed out of her mouth, trying to catch up with her brain to make sense of the nonsensical situation.

"I dinna ken what science is, and I dinna ken half the words you said, but I do understand it as witchcraft. Are ye a witch? You must be a witch. What is it ye want with me?"

His demeanor changed.

"I'm not a witch! I'm a lawyer!" was all she could think to say.

"Are ye workin' with a witch, then?"

"No!" she said. "Well, . . . maybe?"

"Which is it? Make up yer mind, lassie."

"I don't believe in magic or witches or any of that," she said. *Facts. Let's stay with facts.*

"Believe it or not, I went to sleep last night in my uncle's stable and woke up here. Over two hundred years in the future and across the sea."

"Yeah . . . that part is trickier," she said.

They looked at each other, sizing one another up. For as strange as this situation was, something felt . . . normal. Something about him felt familiar. How was that even possible? How would a brutish giant Scotsman standing in front of her make her feel normal?

"Okay . . ." she said. "Let me think. There has got to be a solution." *Of course!* "The ren faire is still in town today. Let's go back and find the woman and have her send you back."

He nodded.

"Okay, I'm going to go up to the house and get dressed, and I'll meet you out front in thirty minutes."

"Thirty minutes?"

Hannah shook her head. "Yes, in a while. Give me time to get cleaned up, and I'll meet you outside of the house up on the hill, and we'll go and get this all cleared up."

This better work, she thought.

"Yes, mistress," he said with a slight bow and a gleam in his eye.

SHE OPENED the garage door to see that he was still there. He was real—flesh and blood—and appeared to be scared of the garage door. Hannah had put on her costume from the day before. She was certain it was too revealing for historical accuracy, "but when you got it, flaunt it at a ren faire," as Poppy had told her.

He looked at her, his eyes almost bugged out of his head.

"I thought what ye previously had on was improper, but I fear you are going to spill right out of that top. I canna let ye leave yer home dressed in such a way, mistress."

"Well, it is a good thing you don't have any say in what I wear—no one does. AND this is not a modern dress. We are going to a ren faire, which is an old-timey fair, and amazingly enough, you won't look out of place at all, so there is that. Now get in," she said, opening the car door.

"Get in what? In that?" he asked, looking confused. His eyes filled with uncertainty.

"Yes, this is my car. Get in."

"I've readied two horses. They wait for us tied to that tree." He gestured over to the tree next to the porch, and sure enough, two horses were saddled and tied to the tree.

"Well, we can't ride horses there, so let's put them back in the stable and ride in the car."

"What is the purpose of owning horses if ye dinna need to ride them?"

"We do ride them, sometimes, but not to go places."

"Ye ride them, but not to go places?"

He looked flummoxed.

"Will you please just get in the car?!" she said, her patience wearing thin. She needed to get this problem fixed.

He looked unsure, but he agreed to take the horses back to the stable.

When Hannah drove her car over to pick him up, he just looked at it. She reached over, pulled the handle on the passenger side, and the door popped open.

"Get in."

His eyes widened. "What exactly is this thing?"

"It's a car. Kind of like a horseless carriage. We'll drive it to the fair."

"And ye ken how to do such a thing?"

"I've had my driver's license since I was sixteen, for growing up in the city, that is a badge of honor. I spent my whole summer out here driving so I could get it. Now, get in."

Looking out of place, he tried to fold his body into the car before shutting the door behind him.

After she turned on the radio, he nearly jumped out of his skin, looking bewildered.

She turned it off. "Okay, quiet drive, it is." She put the car into drive and started down the driveway.

"What kind of magic power is this? How can ye not believe in witchcraft and drive a horseless carriage?"

"Science. I have no idea how it works, but it is a gas-powered engine."

"I dinna ken what those words mean."

"Ya wanna know something funny? I don't, either, but I do know how to drive it, so that's all we need to worry about."

They drove about twenty minutes to the fair site in relative silence, his eyes wide as he took it all in. From time to time, she'd feel him look at her; something about his eyes on her felt good, which was a little unsettling.

They arrived at the fair and searched for Bridget's tent. Hannah looked over at Graham, who didn't look out of place, as people gave him props for his costume. He would give them a confused "Thank ye."

Finally, he turned and asked, "Why do these people all think I'm in a costume?"

"I told you this is not even close to how we dress in modern times, just at this fair."

"Where is this bloody witch . . . ?" he grumbled.

There it was, tucked between a jewelry stand and one selling fairy wings.

"That's it," she said, pointing to the booth.

They headed toward the tent, which was empty when they entered, except for the little old woman, who seemed to be expecting them.

"Ahhh, hello, deary. Back so soon? Looks like ye had some luck with yer spell, then. Ye are a handsome one, aren't ye?" She looked Graham over with an approving nod.

"I'm not sure I would call it luck," said Hannah.

The woman turned to Hannah, raised her eyes, and smiled. "I would say luck. He's what ye asked for, is he not? in yer love spell?"

"Love spell?" Graham raised a brow.

"Wait a minute! I did not ask for a brutish Scotsman from two hundred and fifty years ago. I thought maybe it would help me clear my mind and hone in on what I wanted. I do not want this."

"Well, be that as it may, he's here now," said the woman with finality in her voice.

"But how do I send him back?"

"Oh, I am afraid that is impossible."

"Witch! Send me back to my own time," Graham bellowed, grabbing her shoulders.

"Woah! That is unnecessary," Hannah said as she put her hand on his shoulder, ignoring the electricity that thrummed through her at the touch.

"This is the witch who brought me here, this is the witch to send me back," he said, still holding her tight, turning red with anger and frustration.

The witch did not seem fased by him in the slightest.

"I canna send ye back. The spell was done on the equinox and can only be undone on the equinox," she said, looking him calmly in the eyes.

He let her go with a roar.

"Auch," he said before grumbling other things in Gaelic that seemed anything far from good.

"So, he is here until the next equinox? What does that mean?" Hannah asked.

"It means, in six months' time, under the moon of the spring equinox, ye can work another spell to send him back. That is, if you still wish to do so."

"You mean he is here for six months?"

"Aye, that is what I mean," the woman said with a smile on her face.

"What am I supposed to do with him for six months?"

"I can take care of myself, lass. You dinna need to worry about me," he said, crossing his arms over his chest.

"Well, actually, I do! A lot has changed in two hundred and fifty years. They will lock you up if you don't have help, and I did not ask for a giant man to take care of!" Hannah spat.

"I most certainly do not need a lass to look after me," Graham bellowed.

"Well, I think you two will just have to figure it out," said the woman, calmly.

"Just give me the spell."

"Ye must be quite powerful to bring someone through time and space to ye. That, or the love betwixt ye is powerful enough to bring him to ye."

"The spell please."

Hannah's patience for this woman had ended. She could feel Graham seething beside her, and she was quite angry at him for manhandling the poor woman, as infuriating as she may have been.

She handed Hannah the spell and said, "That will be fifty dollars."

"Fifty dollars! That's robbery! Yesterday, it was twenty."

"Aye, love spells are twenty. These are fifty."

"I don't have fifty dollars on me," she said.

"I take credit," the woman said, pulling out a smartphone and opening an app.

"This is bullshit," Hannah said as she handed her the card.

Graham looked at her, eyebrow raised. The witch handed her back the card and gave her the spell bag.

"It was a pleasure doing business with ye, lass." She smiled.

Hannah stormed out of the tent, Graham trailing behind.

What on earth was she supposed to do? How was she going to explain the sudden appearance of an ancient Scotsman? What was she going to do with him for six months? She was hoping for clarity to help her solve her problem, not compound her problem with this unexplainable situation.

Plus, she had asked for a man she didn't have to take care of. She had to babysit a surly Scotsman who knew nothing of modern time. That would be more work than any of her past boyfriends. Cleaning up after them or always picking up the check was one thing, but the situation yielded a whole other level of care. Anger and resentment bubbled inside her.

Hannah turned to leave. She needed to regroup. She

checked if he was following her. He had stopped and looked back at the witch. The woman winked at him with a knowing smile. He looked confused, and Hannah couldn't blame him. She was still trying to wrap her brain around the day.

He turned to follow her, and Hannah booked it to the car. She needed to get out of there, but her new problem—a large, ancient Scotsman—was following behind her and would for six months.

"Slowdown, will ye? And let's get this sorted," he said, grabbing her arm, swinging her around.

"What is there to sort? This whole thing is ridiculous. I don't understand what happened, and now, we are stuck like this for six months," she said bitterly. She shook her arm free and looked at him.

He gave her a look she couldn't read. She didn't have time for this.

"Let's just go home, and I'll get this all figured out." She turned and headed to the car.

He put his hands on her shoulders and spun her around again. "Now, calm down, will ye? Tell me what happened. Did the witch trick ye?"

"DO NOT put your hands on me like that." She glared at him. "You cannot just manhandle women to get your way in the modern day. We have minds of our own, ya know. You can't just grab us," she shouted.

He dropped his hands from her shoulders and looked at her like she was a puzzle to be put together. "I will not touch ye if ye don't wish to be touched, lass."

"And what about that woman in there? You think you can just shake her until she does what you want?" she shouted.

"That woman is a witch. We burn women like her in my time," he spat back in a harsh whisper.

"Forget it. Let's just go." She turned and walked off, and he trailed behind.

The car ride home was silent. His unease was written on his face when looked at the car like he was riding in a spaceship. She tried to have sympathy for him, but the whole situation was infuriating.

How did this happen? She considered herself to be a logical person, so there was no way this was happening.

He suddenly jumped in surprise when his elbow hit the little lever that rolled down the window. She couldn't help but chuckle.

When they arrived at the house, the sun had sunken into the western side of the sky in the late afternoon.

He hadn't eaten, and his stomach growled.

She looked over at him. "You must be hungry. Let's get something to eat. I'll see what we have in there." She gestured to the house.

"If it is all the same, mistress, I think I might head down to the stables and clear my mind. And then I'll come to join ye for a meal," he said slowly.

She was surprised by his answer. She wasn't sure why, since it was a perfectly reasonable request, and honestly, she could use some space, too.

"Yeah, that sounds okay."

She walked up the stairs and shut the door. So much for figuring out her life, but she was now stuck figuring out what to do with the guy.

Taking a moment, she thought about what he must be feeling. Yes, this was a crazy situation, and his shock had to be extreme. It was a shock to her, and she was still in the world she knew. Everything must have been so different to him. It was hard to imagine what he must have been thinking. What was she going to do?

She took a breath, went upstairs to change out of her

outfit, and put her comfy clothes back on. Figuring it out was all she could do. She couldn't wish it away—it was happening.

He came back to the house as Hannah set out some plates on a table on the porch. She watched him as he walked up the stairs. He was a towering presence. From his height to his build, he was big. He was still wearing his kilt and boots and all his other clothes from the past, but for the first time, she looked past all that. Something about him both unnerved and centered her simultaneously.

He nodded and smiled. Hannah tried to subdue the way that made her feel. Something about that moment felt intimate. It felt like spending time with a man, not a problem to be fixed. That made sense, she supposed, since that is exactly who he was, a man trying to deal with this situation like she was. On top of it all, he was incredibly handsome.

"I wasn't sure what you like to eat, so I figured you can't go wrong with chicken and potatoes, right?" She chuckled and fidgeted with the zipper of her hoody.

He looked at the plate and tilted his head.

"I'm afraid I haven't been able to get to the grocery store. I had to rummage around in the freezer, so we have some chicken strips and some French fries. I cut up some apples from the Smith's orchard, so those are good, at least. Am I feeding you like a toddler? I'm sorry. I never really cook much in the city. I eat a lot of takeout, and one of my best friends in the city's fiancé is a chef, so I eat well in the city. But there wasn't much here yet."

"I'm sure this will fill my belly just fine. Did ye say these were French?" he said, examining the chicken strip.

"Um . . . no, that's chicken. This is a French fry" she said, holding up a crinkle-cut fry from the oven. "Not a very good one, and probably not even French . . . Once again, I apologize for this meal," she said opening a bottle of wine before pouring them each a glass. "You drink wine, right?"

"Have ye no whiskey?"

Hannah shook her head.

"Well, it'll do just fine."

They dug in. He ate, and she watched in amusement as he stabbed the French fries with a fork. She stifled a laugh at his expressions. Then he cut a chicken strip and ate it.

Hannah ate her chicken and fries by dipping them in ketchup. He watched her, then put down his fork, picked up a fry, and dipped it. He then bit into an apple.

Hannah was no stranger to the comfort of food, but she had never seen it written so plainly on someone's face. He was clearly relieved to be eating something familiar.

"Was it terrible?" she asked.

"My belly is filled," he replied.

"Well, that's all that counts, I guess."

The sun had started to set in the sky, and an awkward silence fell between them.

"Well, it has been quite a day, huh?" she said, smiling awkwardly at him.

"Aye."

"So . . . if you want, we have lots of bedrooms here you can sleep in."

"The stable is well enough for me. I can check on the horses, and I will sleep just fine there."

"Oh, okay. Tomorrow, let's talk and get this all worked out," she said getting up to clear the table. "I'm sorry for all of this. I never intended for any of this to happen."

The apology was genuine. She really did feel bad for disrupting his life. He didn't ask for this any less than she did. This whole situation on top of the events of the past week had Hannah's nerves fried.

"Aye, dinna worry. We will figure it out tomorrow." He caught her eye and shared a kind smile.

He stood. "Well, I think I will head back to the stable for the night. Goodnight, m'lady," he said to her with a bow.

"Here. In case you get hungry," she said, passing him two apples.

"Thank ye."

He turned and headed down the path to the stable. Hannah watched him probably longer than she should have. He turned around as he was about halfway to the stable. He smiled at her, and Hannah felt that smile in places she shouldn't have. She shook the feeling and turned to head inside.

CHAPTER 4

*T*he next morning, Graham woke up in the same strange barn. He would be lying if he said he didn't want to wake up in his own time, but there he was, in the future, still trying to wrap his head around what had happened. Some witch had brought him here because of a love spell. That was all he could figure out. Although, he couldn't figure out why a lass like Hannah would need a love spell.

She was beautiful. The first time he saw her in those indecent britches, all he could do was keep from staring at her round, ample backside. Then, when she came out in that corset with her bosom nearly popping out of the top, he fought the urge to pull all that softness against him and kiss her full, pouty lips.

Feeling so out of place and frustrated, he knew he had been gruff with her. He didn't want to be angry, especially not at her, but resentment settled within him. She performed the blasted love spell that brought him there.

He was supposed to be getting ready for the clan gathering back home to decide whether the MacNeil clan would join the rebellion. He had hoped to be marching out to join the cause soon. Instead, he was in a place where nothing made sense and things were so foreign.

After feeding the horses, he walked over to the woodpile behind the barn, ready to chop wood to clear his head. Working on something physical always helped. He never cared much for leisure, so he preferred to keep busy.

After chopping some wood, the sun had chased away the chill in the morning air, and it beat down on him. He slipped off his shirt and kept swinging his ax with all his might, feeling more grounded with each swing.

Footsteps approached the barn. He turned to see Hannah coming around the corner, who carried a cup in one hand and food in the other. She was back in those indecent britches, the loose shirt, and her hair piled atop her head. As she looked at him, her eyes opened wide, and her mouth fell open. Arousal stirred in Graham's body his kilt refused to hide, but at that moment, Hannah tripped over a log. Graham rushed to her side and steadied her.

"Fuck," she called out. She had spilled whatever was in the cup down her shirt. "Well . . . I was bringing you breakfast and coffee, but it looks like you don't get any coffee." She handed him what was in her hand. It appeared to be some type of meat and egg on bread of some kind.

"Are ye all right, lass?" he asked.

"I'm fine," she said, attempting to brush the coffee off her shirt. "There, it's eggs and some bacon on an English muffin."

Graham didn't take his eyes off her; he was waiting to make sure she was okay.

"I'm fine. Eat it before it gets cold."

He took a bite. *Now, this is good*, he thought. The night before, the only thing he had any familiarity with was the apples and wine, but while he had never eaten anything quite like the breakfast, he had the components before, and he was hungry. He wolfed it down and wiped his mouth with the little bit of paper-like fabric she had brought in.

He chanced a glance her way to find her looking at him, mouth parted, her cheeks flushed. Graham liked that look very much—too much. He cleared his throat, and Hannah shook her focus back on his face. Embarrassment danced in her eyes for a moment. He smiled at her. The woman was intriguing.

"Sorry. Okay, so we need to figure some things out if you are going to be here for six months. I figured I'll tell my dad that I hired you to take care of the horses until we can find another stable hand. The only problem is they're coming here next weekend. My whole family is coming in for game day, which is this awful family tradition where we all play stupid field games for a day. It is torture. Anyway, they are going to be here, and they will talk to you. So, I'm hoping to spend some time this week getting you as familiar with this time as possible, if you are okay with that. If not, we can find somewhere else for you to go for the weekend."

"You can hire me? Should I not speak with yer father when he comes?"

Hannah huffed at him and rolled her eyes. "Oh my god, yes, I can hire you. Believe it or not, I am an extremely capable woman, and I'm sure my father believes me to be capable enough to hire a groom."

"I do believe ye to be a capable woman," he said. And he did; he had no doubt she was an extremely capable woman. "I just thought it might be a man's job to hire someone for man's work."

"Man's work?! I will have you know our last groom was a woman."

She had this fire behind her eyes Graham could not get enough of. None of the lasses back home would have dared to talk to him that way, and he liked it. He liked that she didn't shrink away. He caught on to the fact that men and women were more equal in this time, but he still liked Hannah growing all fiery. She seemed so much more alive.

"Well, that's just not proper. I'm glad ye have a man to do it now," he said, only to goad her further.

"Ya know what? Never mind. I will do it. I'll take care of the horses. That was my plan anyway. So, you can just keep chopping wood, and I'll do the work."

"The work of watching me chop wood? I saw the way ye looked at me." He raised one eyebrow, waiting to see the fallout of that comment.

"Excuse me! I do not know what you are talking about—"

"It's all right, lass, I will take care of the horses, although I am certain ye are capable of such. Now, I'm going to go back to chopping wood. You can keep watching, but ye might want to close yer mouth before a wee bug flies in."

Hannah glowered at him. He could see her cheeks reddening. He loved it.

"I was doing no such thing. Come up to the house at dinner, and I will figure out how to teach you about modern times and maybe even modern MANNERS! And you can take a shower. You smell horrible."

She turned and left. Graham tried not to stare at her swaying backside as she walked away. He enjoyed that more than he should have. She was a rare woman indeed.

GRAHAM SAT IN THE KITCHEN, watching Hannah prepare dinner. He was trying to fight the sense of overwhelm he felt from the modern magic. He couldn't describe the other items found inside the house besides magic.

The house was a mix of old and new. On one side of the kitchen was a large fireplace with an old crane. It didn't look much different than the fireplaces in his own time, but on the other side of the room was a large stone table she called an island. Further beyond that was a sink with running water, a very large cabinet to keep food cold, and a stove with self-sustaining fires. A couple of other contraptions were completely foreign to him, but he seemed to get the gist of most things.

He watched the sink as Hannah washed her hands. Running water was, indeed, a miracle, and it was one of the modern conveniences he liked. He had just taken his first shower. The modern bathroom was truly a sight to behold, with magic warm rain and pleasant-smelling soaps. A self-cleaning chamber pot that flushed it all away. Where did it go? He had no idea, but he liked it just the same, even if the sound was a little jarring. He felt the softness of his freshly laundered shirt. Hannah had washed it for him. It had never felt so soft or smelled so nice.

"I'm still not much of a cook, but I ran to the store today to try to make something that might be better for you. I worry that all this modern food and the preservatives in it might upset your stomach. So, I am cooking."

Graham snapped out of his head when she spoke to him. "I'm sure it will taste just fine."

It certainly smelled delicious.

She dished him up some pork chops, roasted potatoes, and green beans. While it was not exactly what he ate in his own time, it was a bit closer to the meal they had shared the day before.

"Poppy brought a pie over from the orchard," Hannah said as she brought out an apple pie.

"This all looks delicious. Thank ye."

They sat at the table. Graham was feeling a little uncomfortable being in the house alone with her. It didn't feel proper. He knew better than to voice that concern.

"It all tastes good. Yer not such a bad cook, after all."

"Well, thank you for that, but I assure you, I'm not a very good cook. This is about as good as it gets, and don't expect this all the time."

They ate quietly, neither of them knowing what to say. When they finished, Graham helped clean up. He brought the dishes over to her as she rinsed them and put them in another cabinet she called a dishwasher.

Things were so convenient. He couldn't help but wonder how people filled their days when so much of the work seemed to be done by magic—or "science," as Hannah would call it.

"So, I've been thinking," Hannah said, "you have to pass for a person from this time for six months. So, I think there are a few things you should know about, and an easy way to teach you might be to watch some movies."

Hannah and Graham spent the next couple of nights eating dinner and watching movies. They watched *Forrest Gump*, some John Hughes movies, *Star Wars*, and *Harry Potter*, for cultural references. *Jurassic Park*, *Schindler's List*, *12 Years A Slave*, and *Apollo 13* to give him a loose working knowledge of history.

Some of these movies were hard to watch. He realized the cruelty of humans never really changed, but he also saw the good parts were still there, like love and family. He enjoyed learning how the world had evolved, but what he was finding the most enjoyable was just simply spending time with Hannah.

"HERE, TRY THESE ON, TOO." Hannah tossed over another pair of pants that landed on Graham's head. They had spent the morning at the mall to get Graham some shoes and clothes. Graham was just about to lose it.

The place was worse than the markets in Paris. He

thought those markets were noisy and crowded, but they were nothing compared to this. Being there assaulted his senses. The overpowering smell of food, the loud sounds piping overhead, the racks of clothes, the people all talking into the wee pocket bricks and hustling about, and how Hannah made him try on countless items of clothing, shirts, pants, shoes, even undergarments. His head was about to burst.

"Graham, do they fit? Do you need a different size?" Hannah asked.

"Hold your horses, woman. I haven't even put on the blasted pants yet," he spat back.

"Okay, well, just let me know. I'm going to go look for some sweaters, it's going to get cold soon."

Graham zipped up the pants and opened the door. She had put him in a wee closet and had just been tossing clothes over the top. He was done. No more.

"Enough. I am done. I am leaving." He stormed to the front of the store. His head was pounding. He didn't know if it was from the noise Hannah had called "music" playing loudly overhead, the too-bright lights, or just being manhandled and bossed about, but he needed to get out of there.

Hannah put her hand on his shoulder.

"You have to take the pants off before you leave," she said curtly.

Graham spun, knocking her hand off his shoulder.

"I will not walk back into the wee closet, woman. I am done. I will not be manhandled or bossed about by ye anymore today!" he shouted.

Peoples' stares burrowed into him, but he didn't care.

Hannah's eyes narrowed.

"We must pay for them. You have to take them off," she said through gritted teeth.

He turned, stomped back in, and took them off. He

stormed out of the fitting room and out of the store entirely, leaving Hannah and the noisy store behind.

He found a quiet bench tucked away and sat, trying to collect his thoughts. Right then, he would rather be back on the battlefields in France than spend another moment in that godforsaken place.

He was also battling the thought of a woman buying him things he couldn't pay for. That thought churned shame deep within him.

He saw Hannah coming out of the store carrying three large bags of clothes. He stood and took the bags from her arms.

"I will find a way to repay ye," he said quietly.

"It's fine," she said, not meeting his eyes.

Graham had the notion things were not fine, but he decided not to press his luck. They made their way to the car, and Graham was relieved when the fresh air hit him.

They didn't speak the whole way home. Graham could tell she was angry, but he was angry, too. So, when they pulled up to the house he headed straight to the barn.

"You are not even going to come in?" she asked.

"I figured that would be the last thing ye wanted."

"You're right." She turned and walked toward the door.

"Why are ye cross with me?" he shouted after her.

"You yelled at me in public. Do you know how embarrassing that is? You can't just treat people like that, Graham."

"Well, I do apologize for embarrassing ye, lass. But do you stop and think how humiliating it is for me to be bossed about, and by a lass, no less, like I canna care for myself? The truth of it is that I canna because I am in a place completely foreign to me. Think how frustrating that is for me in the obscene inside marketplace."

"Graham—"

"No, I apologized for making ye feel bad, but imagine yer

in that movie ye showed me last night. The one with the machine and the men and the woman on those flying things."

"Star Wars."

"Aye, imagine you were in their time, and every time you made a mistake, you were made to feel like you were some kind of monster. Now, I apologize to ye, but just ken I am trying here. Everything is different. It can be disorienting."

"You're right," she said quietly.

"I'm sorry, what did ye say?" He put his hand to his ear. "I clearly misheard you. I thought I heard ye say I was right."

"Stop," she said, glinting a smile. "You're right. I said it. It is hard on both of us, and maybe I could give you a little more grace. I apologize."

He tipped her a curt nod. He needed to get out before the rage deep in his belly released itself on her again. Graham turned and continued back to the barn, and Hannah headed inside. They both needed some time to cool down.

CHAPTER 5

The weekend had come. Her family would be arriving for their reunion and game day. It used to be what they did to celebrate her grandfather's birthday, but after he passed, that family decided to keep up the tradition. Hannah had spent the previous couple of days preparing for the arrival, mentally preparing herself for the shitshow that was game day. Her aunt, uncle, and her three cousins would be coming, along with the rest of her family. Hannah loved her family, but they could be stressful at times.

When they were little, they all stayed at the farm, with all four adults and six kids packed into the farmhouse. Cousins camped out together in the living room, eating popcorn, watching movies, roasting marshmallows for smores at the fire pit, those were some of Hannah's fondest memories.

Now, her extended family would stay at the inn in town, so that relieved stress. It would be her immediate family there for three days, and game day was the whole clan. All of them, beautiful-looking, like the Kennedy's playing football in the yard in Cape Cod . . . then Hannah. At least, that was how she felt.

So, she set things up before they arrived. Grocery shopping, making sure their rooms were ready, making sure everything was tidy, just running down the checklist.

She had been quizzing Graham about pop culture and modern-day equipment and explained her family to him. That weekend was hard enough without dealing with a bizarre past of their new stable hand.

Hannah had wiped down the counters for the third time when Graham came in from the barn. Her parents would be arriving any minute. She decided to go over things with Graham one last time.

"Okay, so do you remember all we have been over about my family?"

"Aye, parents—Richard and Joanna Glenn. Yer brother, Brett, and his wife, Becca, and their children, Bailey and Braxton, and yer younger sister, Josie."

"Good job. And what will you tell them?"

"That I am a friend of Sam's, and I have been helping him stable yer horses, and ye hired me as the new groom."

"Are you sure you still want to do this? It's not too late to back out, stay with Sam and Poppy, or hell, even in the woods, it would seem, until they are gone."

"No, I dinna scare easy. I like a challenge. I have worked in a stable most of my life. I'm sure your father will see me fit for the position."

"Right."

An awkward chuckle escaped her, and she avoided eye contact as she fought the butterflies in her belly. She didn't know why she would let her family get to her that way. They were a loving family for the most part.

Hannah always took on a lot of the responsibility for things because she felt out of place when she was next to her family—it was one of the ways she would try to fit in. Her job as a lawyer had been one of the few things that made her feel like she truly belonged with them, and that weekend, she was going to tell them she had quit her job and no longer wanted to be a lawyer. That thought made Hannah nauseous. What would her father say about that?

"Are ye feeling quite well? Ye seem off," Graham asked.

She could see a tender look of concern in his eyes.

"No, I'm fine."

He inclined his head to her.

She stopped wiping down the counter. "Really, I'm fine. I am nervous about this weekend. I want everything to go smoothly."

Hannah turned when she heard a car pulling up. Her mom and dad got out of the car as the driver unloaded the bags.

She went out to greet them, and Graham followed behind.

"Hi, Mom," she said with a smile.

"Oh, hello, dear. Glad you are here, traffic was awful," her mom said. She leaned over and gave Hannah a kiss on each cheek.

Hannah's dad came over next.

"Where's my Hannah Banana?" he said, then picked up Hannah in a big bear hug.

Richard Glenn was a big man. He was six four and had a large frame that still showed signs of the formidable man he was in his youth, though age and declining health had taken some of that away. Hannah pretended to hate being picked up by his hugs, but deep down, she loved it. They always shared a special relationship. Hannah was not a small person, and her father was the only person to ever attempt to pick her up. She also believed he was the only person who probably could.

"Hi, Dad," Hannah said.

"Have you been enjoying your week here at the farm? We all need to get out of the city sometimes."

"I have. It's been nice."

Graham stood on the porch as Hannah greeted her parents. He had on his new boots, jeans that hugged him in all the right places, and a plain gray T-shirt. His red hair was pulled back, and the sight of him almost took Hannah's breath away. He may have been the most attractive person Hannah had ever seen in real life. She forgot how attractive he was sometimes—because of how much they'd bicker, but every now and then, she would look at him differently.

"Oh, and Dad, Sam introduced me to Graham. He's here from Scotland, and he's looking for a little work. He's good with horses. So, I kind of hired him. See what you think?"

"Sounds good."

Graham walked down to them, strong and steady, with a warm smile on his face. It was not something Hannah was used to seeing.

"Mom, Dad, this is Graham MacNeil."

Richard extended his hand, and Graham met it with a nice, firm handshake.

"Richard Glenn, nice to meet you, Graham."

"Nice to meet ye, too, sir. This is an incredible place ye have here. Ye have some beautiful horses," Graham said.

"Has Hannah taken you out riding on the trails yet?"

"No, we haven't gotten around to that."

"Oh, good. Well, we'll have to do that sometime this weekend."

"Looking forward to it, sir," Graham said.

"Oh, Graham, would you take these bags upstairs? You look like you have some strong muscles," Joanne said. She squeezed Graham's bicep.

"Mother," Hannah protested.

"What? He does, and it's bad for your father's back."

"Aye, it would please me to help ye, ma'am," Graham said.

Hannah could swear his eyes twinkled. Seriously, where was that charm when it came to her? He had won both of her parents over with such ease.

"How's work going? Roger still got that stick up his ass?"

"Yeah . . . he does."

Work talk in less than five minutes—it was going to be a long weekend. How was she going to tell her parents she quit and has no plan on going back . . . ever, if possible? That was a conversation she dreaded.

Joanna and Graham made their way back inside with the bags, and Joanna instructed Graham on which room to take them to.

"Oh, Hannah, your sister missed her flight. Do you think you could pick her up from the airport at 11:30?"

"Mom, that airport is two hours away."

"I know, but there are no trains running that late. Do you mind?"

"Yeah, sure, not a problem. I'll do it."

Hannah's brother had arrived, and Graham had taken all of the bags to their rooms. Her family treating Graham like a servant irritated her. He wasn't there to cater to them. He was supposed to care for the horses.

It was just about time for the campfire. They would roast hot dogs and make smores, a first-night family tradition of the weekend. Carrying wood down to the fire pit, she heard Graham behind her.

"Can I help ye?"

"Oh, sure, just getting ready to start a fire for the kids to roast some hot dogs and marshmallows."

They carried logs from the pile behind the stable to the firepit. Graham started building a fire.

"Ya know, you don't have to do everything they say. You're here to take care of the horses, not be their errand boy. My mom will run you ragged if you don't set some boundaries, and my sister is worse."

"I dinna mind, truly. This is work that I am familiar with. I can take care of horses and lug around heavy things. That doesn't change in any time. I just hope they dinna ask me to make a call on any of those wee pocket contraptions."

He smiled at her, and she tried to deny the little flutter in her chest every time.

"Well, stand back because I have another contraption I haven't shown you yet."

She pulled the lighter from her hoodie pocket and clicked the trigger to ignite a flame.

"What hasn't the future thought of? Though, flint works just as well."

"Do you have a flint?"

He put his hand out. "Let me have a look." He pulled the trigger, and it clicked.

"No, you have to hold it down," she said, showing him the button on the side.

Graham pulled the trigger again, and the flame appeared. He bent down and lit the fire.

"Lighters are a pretty handy thing," she said.

Graham looked at the thing in his hand. "Lighter." He noted the word into his memory bank, shaking his head.

Braxton and Bailey's shrieking laughter came through as they ran toward the group.

Hannah's mother followed. "Oh, Graham, thank you for getting the fire started. Do you mind going up to the house to bring down a little portable table in the garage and some camping chairs?"

"Mom, he is here to stable the horses, not bend to your every whim," Hannah objected.

"Oh, he doesn't mind, do ya, Graham?"

"I dinna mind. I am pleased to help."

Hannah shook her head.

"Oh, Hannah, since I'm with the kids, I set out the hot dogs and marshmallows, could you grab them? And I made a big salad for myself if you want that, instead. I, for one, don't need hot dogs and marshmallows."

Hannah often felt sorry for her mother, she could never make peace with her body. She had been on every diet known to man. She had watched her mother hate her own body since she was a kid. She always ate different meals than the family. She was always in the gym. She went to extraordinary lengths to not have the same body as Hannah. She used to try to get Hannah to go on diets, but more out of something they could bond over rather than to tell Hannah something was wrong with her. But Hannah was not interested in bonding over disordered eating. She would eat what she wanted. She believed it's all about learning how to listen to your body, as it would tell you what it needs, but the outside world was a lot louder than your body sometimes.

"Yeah, I'll run and grab them," she said.

She turned and walked back to the house to get the food.

Graham walked after her.

"I'm so sorry she is treating you like this. You are not here for this."

"Lass, pay it no mind. I can take care of myself. Plus, she asks me nicer than you do."

Hannah stopped, turned, and stared at him. He gave her a devilish smile. Sometimes, she thought he'd tried to make her mad on purpose.

She scoffed, then smirked at him. She couldn't hide her secret delight.

She showed him the table and chairs in the garage. He picked them up and took them down. Hannah followed close behind, with hot dogs, buns, and fixings for smores.

"Before we get back," he said to her quietly, "can ye tell me what exactly is a hot dog?"

The rest of the night was enjoyable. Graham was a natural with the kids and helped them roast the hot dog and marshmallows. Watching him eat a marshmallow for the first time made Hannah laugh. Sweet stickiness covered his mouth. Watching him lick it off his lips did not make her laugh but definitely made her feel something. He was a natural storyteller. Her dad even listened to his ghost stories.

When it was time for the kids to go to bed, everyone walked up to the house and left Graham and Hannah to clean up. Hannah's dad used to help out more, but his health had been declining, which Hannah did not like to think about. She had hoped her siblings would step up and be more helpful, but that was unlikely. That would require her brother to care about anything besides work and her sister to care about anything other than herself, which she didn't see happening anytime soon.

HANNAH SAT IN HER CAR, waiting in the passenger pick-up area, willing her sister to be on time. Her flight had arrived, per the website, so she just needed Josie to get there. Like right then. Or else, she would have to circle the drop-off zone again. Thankfully, Hannah spotted her and honked. Josie picked up her bags and headed to her.

Hannah popped the trunk, and Josie plopped in her bag and ran around to the passenger seat.

"Hi, Han. Thank you so much for coming to get me. I can't believe I missed my flight, I told Mom that I shouldn't fly before noon because I just can't get to the airport before that, ya know?"

"I guess ... How was your flight?"

"It was good."

"No boyfriend this time?"

"Nope, flying solo. I'm sure Mom will have something to say about that."

"She has something to say about everything these days."

Josie lived in LA and had become thoroughly west coast in contrast to her east coast family. She had planned to become an aspiring actor, model, and yoga instructor. It changed every week, which was her prerogative.

Hannah had prided herself in taking no money from her dad and turned down a job offer at his firm. She wanted to do it all on her own. She tried not to be resentful that her siblings did not.

Her brother got his start-up money from their dad, and Josie lived off his money across the country. Hannah knew of a certain level of martyrdom to her relationship with her family, but she was also scared because, if she didn't do it all, who would?

On the drive home, Josie talked about her new passion. She was apparently going to open an aerial arts studio in West Hollywood. And for the first time, Hannah actually hoped she would. Someone in this family needed to be living their best life.

HANNAH WOKE up the next morning groggy from being up so late. She made Graham breakfast and found him walking the horses to the pasture. He met her back at the barn, and she gave him a breakfast sandwich she had thrown together.

"Aye, thank ye, lassie," he said before he took a bite.

"Two more days until they all clear out," she said, more for her benefit than his.

"What in the devil is she doing?" Graham asked with a look of bewilderment on his face.

Hannah followed his gaze and saw her sister out in the sun, yoga mat unfurled, twisting herself up in knots.

"That's yoga . . . and that's my sister, Josie."

"Yoga? 'Tis not decent," he said, shaking his head.

Hannah was not in the mood for his masculine old-world bullshit.

"It is perfectly decent. We have been over this. Women are free to do what they want, wear what they want, and say what they want."

"I hear ye," Graham said. He turned to head back into the barn, then stopped for one last look at Josie. For some reason, Hannah wanted to scream—and not at all out of jealousy because that would be silly.

"All right, well, I am heading back to the house."

Graham gave her a confused look, the same confused look as when she'd get short with him. She didn't have time for it. She had to try to figure out how she was going to tell her dad and the rest of her family about quitting her job and wanting to be a writer. Although, right then, she was having a hard time remembering why she wanted to live there. The tranquilness it usually gave her was a thing of the past, and she was wound as tight as she was in the city.

She walked into the kitchen. She had only been gone a few minutes before her mom took over the kitchen.

"Oh, good morning, Hannah. I am making breakfast. How about some sautéed spinach and egg whites?"

"As tempting as that sounds, I've already eaten," she said.

"Suit yourself. Oh, and don't forget, we have field day games at ten o'clock sharp."

"I won't forget, Mom," Hannah said.

CHAPTER 6

*T*en o'clock came around, and everyone was on the field. Game day was the only planning her brother would do for the family—planning for that day was all him, and Hannah would have loved to skip it. She hadn't inherited the athletic ability the rest of her family possessed. Nonetheless, she made her way to the field.

She saw her father sitting in a chair talking to his sister and her husband. Joanne was wearing a pink track suit, chasing after the kids. Her brother was catching up with their cousins. Even though they all lived relatively close, with the exception of Josie, this was usually the only time of year they all got together.

Speaking of Josie, she didn't see her anywhere.

Then she spotted her walking to field hanging onto . . . Graham's arm. What the hell?

"What's going on?" Hannah said as she approached her family.

"Oh, nothing but you going down." Brett flexed at her.

"Yeah . . . I go down every year, Brett. It's not new. I was referring to you," she said, turning to Graham.

"Oh!" Josie piped up. "Dad is not feeling well, and since I broke up with Paolo and came alone, the numbers are uneven. Graham didn't look too busy in the barn, so I roped him into being on my team." She rubbed his arm.

Hannah was so mad she could spit. "He is an employee. Seriously. You guys have so much nerve!"

"Geez, Hannah, chill out," Brett said.

Nothing made Hannah's blood boil more than being told to "chill."

Graham looked at her tentatively. "If I am interrupting a family tradition, I do have some work I can do in the stable."

"Nonsense," Joanne said. "We are uneven for team sports with Richard's back. We need another. That settles it."

"Fine," Hannah said, seething.

"Hey, babe, ya wanna go grab the cooler? It's got my electrolytes in it," Brett called to Becca.

"Sure thing. Be right back." She jogged off to the house.

"First up is the relay race," Brett yelled, then split them into teams.

And so it started: Hannah's least favorite day of the year.

The day went on with races, tug of war, kickball, and wood-splitting. Hannah had particularly enjoyed wood-splitting. Richard had always won every year until Brett claimed that title a couple of years prior. Hannah secretly suspected he found a way to practice, even though he lived in a Connecticut suburb. But that year, it wasn't even a close competition. Graham almost tripled Brett's wood count. It looked like Josie had found a ringer, and she seemed to be quite pleased with her find.

The last event of the day was the potato sack race. It was almost over. A shower awaited Hannah, then wine and a steak dinner. She just had to get through it.

Shoving her leg in the bag with her mother, Hannah

overheard Josie flirt with Graham next to her. Could this please just be over?

"You could probably just carry me and do all the walking. You certainly are strong enough," Josie said, feeling his arm for the hundredth time that day.

"I dinna believe that is in the spirit of the race, lass. Though I have never done this before."

Josie giggled. Hannah fumed.

"Come on, Hannah, work with me. One leg, then the next," her mother said next to her.

"Yeah, Mom, I know we have done this every year my whole life, no matter how much I hate it."

"Come on, Hannah, this is fun." Her mom smiled at her as they shuffled across the field.

They were the last to cross the finish line. No surprise there, but before they reached it, Hannah had accidentally stepped into what felt like a gopher hole, causing her to fall and bring her mother down on top of her. At that moment, Hannah could not decide whether she was angry or embarrassed or actually hurt, but she was just about to blow.

"Oh, Hannah." Her mother chuckled as she tried to free herself from her bag.

She heard her siblings laughing and her dad inquiring about their well-being, but Hannah was so mad she wasn't seeing straight.

She was aware of a large hand helping her and her mother to their feet.

Joanna walked off, laughing, while Hannah tried to gather herself.

"Are ye hurt, lass?" Graham's soft voice tickled her ear.

"I'm just fine," she said, brushing the grass from her leggings.

"Are we done now? Can this, for the love of God, please just be over now?" Hannah yelled at her family.

Hannah marched toward the house. As she took the first step on her ankle, searing pain shot up her leg, which nearly buckled under her. She felt Graham's strong arms around her waist supporting her.

"Ye're hurt. Let me help ye to the house," he said. He examined her, his eyebrows pinched with concern.

"I am fine! If you will just let go of me, I can do it myself!"

He let go of her. She took another step, willing herself not to limp through the searing pain in her ankle. She failed at not limping but was able to make her way back to the house. She could feel Graham's concerned eyes on her the whole way.

"Walk it off," her brother called.

"Oh, she'll be fine, Graham. What a sweetheart you are for trying to help," her mother said.

Footsteps followed, and she saw her dad approach. He was a man of a few words, but they understood each other.

"I'm fine, Dad."

"I know you are."

"You don't have to follow me."

"I know I don't"

"Could you stop?"

"Humor me."

They walked back silently to the house. By the time she arrived, her ankle was killing her. She stopped at the porch, looked at the stairs, then looked at her dad. He looked back at her with his patient expression and held out his hand. She let out a sigh and took his hand.

"You shouldn't be helping me. You have a bad back."

"My back is strong enough to help you up these stairs."

He got her up the porch stairs and up the stairs to her room so she could relax, shower, and have some time to cool down.

She needed that.

. . .

HANNAH HOBBLED DOWN to the patio to eat dinner with her family. They had one nice meal together that weekend. Hannah usually helped make it, but everyone left her alone that afternoon, after her little outburst at the end of game day. That really wasn't like her. Hannah had decided to tell her family about quitting her job as a lawyer after dinner.

Her brother talked about his job; Becca talked about the kids, who were already inside, calming down with a movie. Josie talked about the studio she wanted to open and her business plan, which she probably made up on the spot. The rest of the family talked about their jobs, and the cousins reminisced about game days growing up. Altogether, the meal was enjoyable.

"Do you want any help cleaning up before we head out?" asked her aunt.

"Oh, don't worry about that. We can get it. It was wonderful catching up with you."

They all said their goodbyes, and her aunt and uncle cleared out. The clock was ticking on Hannah sharing her news.

Joanna started clearing the dishes.

"I'll take care of it, Hannah," she said to her with a smile, like she was doing her a favor, like she didn't have two other children capable of helping her with the dishes.

"Mom, you have two other kids. Brett or Josie can help with dishes."

"Nope, me and Becs have to do bedtime. It's a family ritual," Brett protested.

"Fine, I will do the dishes with Mom. What crawled up your butt, Hannah?" Josie asked.

It looked like it was now or never.

"Okay . . . well . . . I just have something I want to tell you guys. I quit my job."

Everyone stopped and looked at her.

"Roger's an ass. There is always a job for you at my firm, Banana," her dad said with a small smile.

Hannah took a breath. "I don't think I want to be a lawyer anymore."

Her mom gasped, like she had just said someone had died.

"I will figure it out. I just need some time," Hannah said.

"Take some time, Banana. But you can't throw it away. You're a good lawyer. You'll get a better job."

"I know I'm a good lawyer, Dad. But I don't love it. I don't want to do it anymore."

"Do you think I love being a lawyer all the time?" he said in a rare, stern voice. "It is a job. And a damn good job. It has given this family everything it has. Jobs aren't always fun, Hannah. That's why they call them jobs."

Hannah felt like she had been slapped in the face. "Dad, I know. I just don't want to do it anymore."

"Well . . . what exactly is it you plan on doing now?"

"I don't know. I am figuring that out."

"Hannah, you can't just quit your job with no plan."

"I just need some time to figure out my next step."

"Okay, take some time but then come work for me. I think it's best."

She had expected pushback from her dad. He loved that she followed in his footsteps. This had been her way of belonging. Sure, she could go to another firm, find another job as a lawyer somewhere else in the city. But she was ready for a change. She was ready to stop being so stressed about everything all the time. She was ready to leave the world of corporate law and the unrelenting pace of city life.

"I don't think that's best. I want to make my own decisions about my life. I'm not sure I've ever really done that."

"No one forced you to become a lawyer, Hannah. You chose that on your own."

"I didn't, though. I did what was expected of me. I never

truly examined what I actually wanted."

"Where is all this coming from?"

"I just don't want to do it. Don't you ever get tired of being the bad guy? Don't you ever get tired of helping companies screw over people?"

"Is that what you think I do? Screw over people?"

"All I'm saying is that I don't want to be that person anymore. I am tired of working so hard and feeling bad about it."

"I see," Richard said, pushing his chair away from the table. He headed inside.

Joanna and Josie busied themselves with the dishes. She knew she had gone too far.

She was at the table with only her brother, who leaned over and said, "Quite the epic fall from grace this weekend, sis. Favorite child status, here I come. Do I get a raise?" He looked at her.

She knew he was trying to be funny in his own way, but she was still about to punch him. His face softened.

"Just give him some time," Brett said.

"Hey Brett, can you come help me with bedtime?" Becca called down from an upstairs window.

And, just like that, Hannah was alone on the patio. She stood, grabbed a half empty bottle of wine, and headed down to the fire pit. Then she thought better and grabbed another bottle of wine.

CHAPTER 7

*G*raham was bedding the horses for the night. He was about ready to shut off the lights and go to bed on the cot in the office when he looked and saw flames burning in the fire pit. Only one person sat at the fire, and he could tell it was Hannah. He knew she had had a rough day. And even though she had yelled at him, he still wanted to see if she was doing all right.

He walked up to the fire, threw on another log, and sat down next to her.

"I saw ye sittin' here all alone, so I thought ye might like some company."

"Think again," she bit back.

He got up to leave.

"No, I'm sorry, stay . . . I mean, if you want to."

"I wouldn't have walked over here if I dinna want to."

"What a day . . . . what a fucking day," Hannah said, on the cusp of a slur.

Graham looked down and picked up the empty wine bottle next to Hannah.

"It's fine. I have more right here," she said. "Have a drink."

"Aye, I think you have had enough for the both of us." He smiled at her.

She gave him a dirty look. "What are you, the booze police?"

"I dinna reckon I am."

"Well, have a drink, so I'm not drinking alone."

He looked at her and sipped from the bottle.

"I really fucked up," she said.

"How do ye reckon?" he asked.

"I threw a fit at stupid game day . . . which is stupid. Game day is stupid. I sprained my stupid ankle, and I quit my stupid job. And now my family thinks I'm stupid. And really, they should. I mean, I'm the one to quit my stupid job. And now what? I am going to live here and be a writer and bring back an ancient Scotsman for my sister to hit on. That's just my life now . . . stupid . . . so fucking stupid."

"Yer not stupid. Yer one of the least stupid people I have ever known. Game day . . . that may be stupid, but not you."

"I quit my job. Why did I quit my job?" Her voice cracked at the end.

Graham fought his urge to wrap her in his arms and comfort her. "I canna answer that, but I can say ye seemed fairly certain of yer decision until tonight, so I reckon ye should sleep on that one."

"I'm sorry I brought you into this mess. I really hoped you could just take care of the horses until it was time to get you back to your time."

"I can take care of myself, lassie. Yer family dinna make me do anything I dinna want to do, except maybe hop around in a sack with yer sister."

"I don't see why you wouldn't like it. Most men would like to hop around in a sack with my sister. She's the pretty one, and I'm the dependable one, the sturdy one." Hannah patted her stomach, but not really for his benefit.

Graham enjoyed Hannah's biting sarcasm, but it felt different, and he didn't care for it one bit. How on earth could this woman not know how amazing she was?

"Well, I dinna like it, and I dinna think she is the bonny one."

Hannah turned to him, trying to parse the meaning of that remark. Their eyes connected, and it felt like a spark danced between them. Hannah bit her lip. Something stirred inside Graham. He broke eye contact, changing the subject before losing control by claiming that pouty bottom lip she had between her teeth.

"I did like beating yer brother in wood-splitting, though," said Graham.

A broad grin crept across her face. That smile settled deep in him. He wished he could make her smile like that all the time.

"Ya . . . that was pretty great." She chuckled. "He was so pissed."

They sat in silence, looking up at the stars.

"But really, I am sorry for bringing you here," she said in a serious tone. "I mean, like, all the way here. I never intended for that to happen. It was just supposed to be a love spell to bring me love and help me to figure out things. Instead, I messed up both of our lives. You've been great . . . mostly." She flicked him a small smile.

Graham held onto that smile; it felt like something real.

"You've handled waking up two hundred and fifty years in the future better than I've handled you being here."

"Dinna worry about me, lass. Ye did me a favor. I was about to leave to fight the Red Coats with my uncle, and this is far more enjoyable than that."

"You were going to fight the Red Coats? As in, the British?"

"Aye, the day I woke up here, my clan was to decide on

whether we would join the rebellion to fight to bring back the rightful king to the throne. My uncle is the war chieftain of the clan. He thought we should answer the call to arms. The chief was not so sure. If they had decided, I would be marching out now to join troops for battle."

"Wow, that sounds more intense than game day."

"Aye, but some things are worth fighting for," he said, keeping his eyes on the fire.

"Have you been in battle before?"

"Aye, I fought in France before I returned to Scotland to aid in the cause."

He looked at Hannah to see her looking at him in a way he had never seen before. He chalked it up to the copious amount of wine she had consumed.

They returned to the comfortable silence, and she returned to stargazing. He watched her. The fire illuminated her face, highlighting her beautiful features. She was beautiful since the moment he saw her. He had wanted to protect her, but she didn't need anyone to protect her. Women in the modern time baffled him. Girls like Josie, he understood; they had those in his time. But Hannah, with her fierce independence and a sharp tongue, intrigued him. It baffled him how she seemed to cower with her family until that afternoon. Though she was upset, he loved to see the fire back in her eyes, even when directed at him.

"Ummm, Graham," she said in a sleepy, slurry voice. She turned and looked at him. "I don't think I can make it back to the house."

He got out of his chair and moved over to her. He bent down and lifted her twisted ankle.

She winced as he touched it. "I think I sprained it, and I have just been, 'spite walking on it all afternoon."

It was twice its normal size, and even by the firelight, Graham could see the bruising setting in.

"All right, lassie, up ye get. Let's get ye into bed."

He offered her a hand and helped her out of the low Adirondack chair. He put one arm around her back and bent down to put the other around her legs.

"What do you think you are doing? I can walk!" she protested.

"Actually, I dinna think ye can."

"Just help me a little," she instructed.

She put some weight on her ankle and hissed.

"Just let me carry ye," he said.

"You can't pick me—"

Graham swept her up into his arms and walked up to the house.

"You can't carry me. I'm too heavy," she said, her eyes wide.

"It appears as though I can carry ye, lass. I'm strong enough for that."

He looked into her eyes, which were mere inches from his own, her mouth parted. Graham reminded himself and his cock that she was drunk and injured. So, they needed to calm down.

It was quiet inside. Everyone was in their rooms.

He made it up the stairs and whispered, "Which room is yers?"

"The last one."

The sweet smell of wine and the heat on her breath brushing his ear deepened his desire to be close to her.

He opened the door and set her on the bed. He found the light switch and turned it on. He noticed how flushed she looked. He removed her shoes and socks, being very delicate with her injured ankle. In the light, it looked painful. It had puffed into a deep purple bruise that pooled at the base of her ankle.

"What can I do to ease the pain?" he asked.

"Can you get me an ice pack? Little plastic baggy with ice and a towel."

"Aye . . . I will go see what I can find in that magical place ye call a kitchen."

He got up to leave, but she took his hand. His heart pounded at her touch. The desire he had been keeping at bay threatened to overtake him, but he would make no move in her current state.

"Hey . . ." she muttered. "Thank you."

He nodded at her and turned to leave, but she still clung to his hand. He turned to look at her. A haze took over her face. He looked at her, seeing her in a new way. He wasn't used to seeing vulnerability in her eyes.

"You are beautiful," she said.

He wasn't sure she meant to voice it aloud, but there it was. A small confirmation that she saw him the way he saw her. His thumb grazed her fingers.

"Aye, now let me go get ye that ice pack."

He made his way back down to the kitchen but realized he was not alone. Josie was in the kitchen.

"Graham, what are you doing here?"

His heart raced. In his time, had someone seen him coming from a woman's bedroom in the middle of the night, it would have ended in a beating or a wedding, neither one he wanted to deal with. He reminded himself that modern times were different, but he was still glad it was Josie and not Mr. Glenn, since he couldn't imagine times were *that* different.

"Hannah was having trouble getting up the stairs. She hurt her ankle very badly. I was going to take her an ice pack."

"Oh, I can do that. Don't trouble yourself."

"No trouble at all, lass."

"No, I will take it to her."

He didn't want to leave, but he was not going to argue with her.

"Aye." He nodded. "Good night."

"Wait a minute," Josie said, taking him by the hand.

What was it with the women in this family taking him by his hand? His heart raced when Josie did it, too. Not with desire, like it did with Hannah, but more panic. He was in a precarious place. He didn't want to rock the boat and be sent away. Where would he go?

"We made a good team today, don't you think," she purred.

"Aye, we did. Excuse me, miss."

"You're so proper and cute. Call me Josie." She looked at him and ever so slyly licked her lips.

"Aye, miss Josie, can ye take yer sister and ice pack? I've got to be gettin' back to the horses." He took back his hand, then turned on his heel and left the kitchen.

CHAPTER 8

*H*annah was lying on her bed, her head spinning from the wine. Did she just tell Graham he was beautiful? Surely, that was a wine-induced hallucination. A quiet knock tapped the door.

"Come in." She was expecting an undeniably attractive Scotsman to be standing at the door with some concoction he would call an ice pack. Instead, it was her sister with an actual ice pack.

"Hey, Han, I heard you needed this."

"Oh, yeah, thanks."

Josie brought it to the bed and laid it on her ankle.

"Oh my god, Hannah! Your ankle looks awful!"

"Feels awful, too."

"Why didn't you say it was this bad?"

"It's fine. Just give me the ice pack."

"Okay. I was talking to Graham in the kitchen. I think he's cute."

"Oh, yeah?" Hannah clenched her teeth.

"I mean, yeah! Don't you think? And the accent . . . delicious! And, Hannah, did you see him chopping that wood? I think I might sneak into the barn tonight. Is he sleeping in the office?" A sly smile crept across her face.

"Josie!" Hannah sat up. "You can't do that!"

"What? Why not?"

"He's an employee! That's harassment!" Hannah protested.

"Oh, Hannah, lighten up. I'm not going to accost him . . . just let him know I'm an option," she said, evaluating herself in the mirror.

"Josie, no, you can't." Hannah's heart raced. She shook her head.

Josie looked over her sister. "Oh my god, how did I not see this? You like him."

"I do not," Hannah bit back.

"Oh, you totally do!"

"I don't know what you are talking about."

"Yes, you do. I say go for it. You are doing a whole Hannah-getting-her-groove-back thing right now, and if a bonafide hotty with a Scottish accent is part of that, I am one hundred percent behind you."

"Josie, you're being ridiculous."

"I am not, and you know I'm not." She flicked her sister a knowing glance. "Anyway, it's your call. He's all yours."

"You're crazy." Hannah's heart recovered, but she couldn't look her sister in the eye.

"Good night, Hannah, I love you and your decade-early mid-life crisis." She put her hand on Hannah's knee, waiting for her to look at her.

"Good night, Josie. I love you and your absolutely insane and untrue observations."

Josie turned off the light as she left. She closed her eyes, trying to find sleep. She had just enough wine that she didn't have to replay the event of the day in her head. Something she was thankful for, though, was something she would probably kick herself for in the morning.

HANNAH WOKE up the next morning, head-splitting, ankle throbbing, feeling like she would sell her soul for a glass of water. She reached over and looked at her phone. It was already 10:30 a.m. Her mother would have never let her sleep this late. She listened for the hustle and bustle of the house. She knew her brother and his wife and kids were probably gone already, but she figured everyone else was probably getting ready to go. She dragged herself to sit up. Then she saw a little note on her nightstand.

Daddy wanted to miss traffic, so we left early. We are taking Josie to the airport.

Lots of love

Mom

Hannah had hoped to make things right with her dad that morning. Hannah and her mom always had a tenuous relationship, but she had always had a special relationship with her father. It didn't feel right, and in all honesty, she was upset they had left her in such a condition. Given they really had no idea how sincerely fucked her ankle was, she was irritated nonetheless.

She attempted to get out of bed and head to the bathroom. She stumbled into her dresser. She caught herself but not before knocking over half of the items on top of the dresser with a crash.

"Shit!"

She held onto the wall and tried to hobble herself to the bathroom.

As footsteps behind her approached, she turned to see a head of red hair coming up the steps. He silently walked over to her and helped her to the bathroom. She fought the urge to refuse help because maybe she did need it for once.

"Thank you," she mumbled.

He nodded and looked at her, the corner of his mouth upturned.

She went into the bathroom. After finishing, she looked in the mirror. Her hair looked like a bird's nest on top of her head, her eyes red and rimmed with dark circles, with a tiny touch of crusted drool on her chin. Lovely. She cringed knowing Graham had seen her like this, then she remembered some of their interaction last night with a similar cringe.

Had she called him beautiful? Did he really carry her full weight? Had her sister accused her of having a crush on him? She wanted to crawl under a rock for about—oh, six months should do it. Since quitting her job at Mr. Glass's office, reality had swept her away. At first, it was exhilarating, but since then, she just felt battered by the storm.

She washed her face and brushed her teeth. After attempting to brush her hair, she gave up and put it back up in a bun. She found the ibuprofen and downed a couple, mentally preparing herself to hobble back to her room. Graham had been waiting with an ice pack in hand.

"Yer sister told me ye might need this when ye woke up. She also said I should take ye to the doctor, but if ye were stubborn to tell ye, at least to call Jackson to come to look at ye."

"I'm fine," she grumbled. She took his help back to her room.

"Yer hurt," he said firmly. "Let people help ye. At least call Jackson, whoever he is, like yer sister said."

"Fine."

She knew she was being short-tempered with the wrong person, but she couldn't help herself. "Let people help you."

Graham's words rattled around in her head. Letting people help her was not something she did well or often.

"I am going to go get ye some breakfast. Are ye comfortable up here, or would ye rather go downstairs?"

"This is fine."

"Well, I'm glad it's fine," he said in a gentle mocking tone before smiling at her.

Hannah—though she was in pain, irritated, and feeling out of sorts—smiled back. A real smile.

When he left, Hannah reached for her phone to text Poppy.

Hannah: This weekend sucked. Game day blew up and when I told my dad I quit my job he left dinner and, then left completely without saying goodbye. Also, my ankle is fucked . . . please send Jackson or else Graham might insist I go to the doctor and let's face it, if I go to the doctor they will just tell me to lose weight even though a sprain is my problem and after quitting my job I don't have bail money.

Poppy: I will be over on my lunch break and Jackson will come over when he gets off work. Sorry this weekend was such a shit show. I'll bring some Twistee's for lunch, chili dogs and cherry-limeades fix everything.

Hannah: Thanks, you're the best.

Poppy: I know

After knocking on the door, Graham opened it slowly. He came in, holding a tray that had a mug of coffee, some scrambled eggs and toast, and a small bowl of fresh strawberries. Hannah couldn't help but smile. No one had brought her breakfast in bed since she got her tonsils out in the seventh grade.

"Wow, you made all of this? How did you make all of this?"

"I believe the words yer looking for is 'thank ye, Graham,'" he said with a smile on his face.

"Yes, thank you, but also, I have had boyfriends from this time who couldn't have managed a breakfast like this. And here you are, in the modern day, for barely over a week mastering the coffee machine," she said as she straightened up in her bed. She took a sip of the coffee.

"Well, yer sister set that up before she left. All I had to do was push a wee button she showed me. I've watched ye make these eggs before, so I had your sister show me how to get the fire in your kitchen so I could make these for ye."

"Thank you, Graham. I mean it."

He nodded and leaned against the door frame, watching her intently.

"I have the horses fed and out in the pasture already, so I am here for anything ye need today."

"Thanks, I should be good."

"Nonetheless, I am here. Do I need to call this Jackson fellow? I will need yer help with the . . . calling contraption . . . that one still eludes me."

"No, I texted Poppy, she is coming over in a bit. You've met Poppy and Sam. Jackson is Sam's boyfriend, he is a nurse, so he'll come and look at it."

"Sam's boyfriend?" he asked.

"Yes, his boyfriend. And don't you dare be weird and rude about this." She shot him a chilling look.

He put his hands up. "Not going to be rude. Just clarifying. We had people with the same proclivities back in my day. They were just hung for it if the wrong people knew."

"Well, they aren't anymore. They are just as valid as anyone," Hannah snapped.

"I didn't say they weren't, lass. I didn't care in my day, so I'm not about to start now," he said.

"Okay . . . . two hundred years changes a lot of things," she said.

"That is certain, but many things are still the same," he

said. He walked over to the bed, looked under the ice pack, then touched her ankle. "Does it hurt much? I dinna like seein' ye in pain."

"It's okay, as long as I don't walk on it." Hannah noticed the sensation of his touch on her ankle, and even the pain couldn't block out the pleasant feeling it brought.

"Ye should try and get some rest," he said as he took the breakfast tray. "Please, let me know if ye need anything, lass." He gave her a genuine, piercing look.

Hannah lost her words, and all she could do was nod.

Graham turned and left the room. She heard his steady footsteps head down the stairs.

Crap, Hannah thought to herself. She was in trouble. She had been attracted to him from the moment she saw him—physical attraction she could easily deny herself. This . . . this felt different. No one had taken care of her like that. She had never let anyone take care of her like that, but she could tell it was different with him. He was going to take care of her, whether she liked it or not . . . and she did like it . . . more than she cared to admit.

THAT AFTERNOON, as promised, Poppy came over with lunch for everyone.

"Jackson is going to bring you some crutches and check on you when he gets off work," Poppy said.

Hannah nodded, taking a sip from her cherry limeade.

"So, what happened with your family? Why did they leave so early? I thought they were staying another day."

Hannah sighed, her eyes drifting to the note on her nightstand.

"They were going to, but Josie needed a ride to the airport, and Dad wanted to beat traffic, so they drove home early."

"Is he pissed that you quit your job?" Poppy asked, then shoved a cheese fry in her mouth.

"I don't think so. He offered me a job at his firm again, and I told him no and then I told him I didn't want to be a lawyer anymore. And then I maybe implied that he screwed people over for a living. I think that's what did it. Sure, he wants me to be at his firm, but he always kind of respected my need to do things on my own. I mean, he basically supports my sister and started my brother's business. All I am asking for is some time, and he's acting like he knows what's best for me."

"Man . . . that sucks."

"Yeah, and because I refused to let them know how hurt I actually was, they all left, and now, I am here with this." She gestured to her ankle, which was still purple and twice its normal size.

"Yeah, that's gross." Poppy examined her ankle.

Hannah laughed and gave Poppy's arms a push.

"Well, Jackson will be over to check it out. And in the meantime, you seem to have a hot, doting highlander in your living room just waiting to help you," Poppy said, giving her a knowing look.

"Yeah, he's actually been really great, which is weird." Hannah bit back a smile creeping across her face, but if she gave any signs of attraction, Poppy would pounce.

"It's not that weird. I mean, you did a magic spell to bring your perfect man, and he appeared."

Hannah hit her again, this time a little harder.

"Poppy, stop it. It's not like that."

"Oh, no . . . it is totally like that. I see the way you look at him."

"I mean . . . yeah . . . he's hot but also infuriating." Hannah shoved away any notion that the flush creeping up her neck to her cheeks was from anything but anger.

"So, my friend, are you," Poppy said before popping one last fry in her mouth, looking far too smug.

"He was really great with my family this weekend, though . . . , and he has taken care of me with my ankle and when I was drunk last night—"

"Hold on, you got drunk last night?"

"Yeah . . . after the fight with my dad. I may have drunk a bottle of wine. And he may have carried me up to bed since I couldn't walk. It's all kind of a blur."

She left out the part where she called him beautiful. That was going with her to the grave.

Poppy sat up straight. "What? How do you leave this part out of the whole story?"

"Because it is embarrassing, Poppy, and you won't let me forget anything, even things I want to forget."

"Well . . . isn't that what best friends are for? That and to help you realize that you are into him."

"Shut up and stop acting like we are sixteen and having a sleepover." Hannah's phone buzzed on her nightstand. She picked it up. "It's Sadie, she just heard that I broke up with Andy and wants to know now if I am still planning on bringing a plus one to her wedding . . . crap. I need a plus one to get through a wedding with my old coworkers."

Hannah: Yep! I have a new date.

Sadie: Great! See you in 2 weeks.

Hannah dropped her phone on the bed beside her, put the pillow over her face, and groaned.

"Crap! Do you think Sam would be my plus one?"

"Hannah, you have a hot plus one sitting in your living room right now. Can you imagine the look on their faces when you show up with a guy looking the way he looks?"

That thought did appeal to Hannah. Graham was excessively good-looking, and the thought of dancing with him at a wedding made her feel a certain type of way.

"I couldn't do that . . ."

"You could."

"No."

"Yes."

"Do you think?" Hannah asked.

"Hannah, YES! I think. Do it! You clearly like him, and he would be a good screw-you-old-bosses-look-how-awesome-my-life-is-now kind of date," she said.

"Well, the first part is not true, but the second part is definitely true."

"Both parts are true," Poppy said, looking her square in the face.

Hannah envisioned the look on her boss's face when she showed up with him. And she may have been imagining dancing with him and feeling those muscles of his under a dress shirt, and that thought may have had her heart racing a little. She already had the dress—and, well, Graham wasn't busy . . . so.

"Maybe I will," she said, still picturing it.

"I hate to do this, Han, but I gotta get back to the register. Jackson will be over around five. Do you need anything before I go?"

"Nope, I'm all good."

Poppy gave her a quick hug.

"I'll check on you later."

"Bye."

Hannah listened to her footsteps head down the stairs. When she heard the door shut, she slumped back onto her bed and closed her eyes. Should she ask him to the wedding?

A small knock followed.

"Come in," she called.

Graham opened the door. "I just wanted to see if you needed anything. It looks like it might storm, so I am going to go stable the horses."

"Nope, I'm good . . . except I do have a favor to ask you."

He regarded her with the half smile that appeared on his face so often.

"I'll do anything ye ask, lass."

"Well, in that case."

CHAPTER 9

*E*very night involved watching more movies, more learning about the modern world. He continued to take care of Hannah while her ankle healed, and he was happy to see some changes. They set into an easy rhythm, with Hannah writing all day while her ankle healed and Graham taking care of the horses.

For the first few days after Hannah's injury, Graham waited on her, took over meal prep, and helped her around. Even though she had crutches, Graham preferred helping her. She was reluctant at first, but eventually, she gave in, and they were starting to find comfort in each other's company.

Over the weeks, Hannah's ankle healed, but they were still spending most of their time together. Hannah had been trying to prepare him for the wedding and for the city.

Graham was nervous about the city. With how the movies portrayed the city, he could never have dreamed up a place like that, but he would experience it soon enough.

When they arrived in the city, Hannah hailed an Uber with her phone. Graham was constantly amazed at what that little thing could do. He didn't understand how electricity worked, but he liked it just fine. Indoor plumbing, he would sorely miss when he returned to his own time. Even cooking in the kitchen was getting easier. But for the life of him, Graham could not figure out the phone Hannah kept in her pocket. She had even bought him one, but he had no clue how to use the thing.

Despite seeing the city in the movies he watched with Hannah, nothing could have prepared him for it. It was loud and crowded, no green to be found anywhere. He was unsettled by the honking of car horns and the sounds of construction. His hand reached for the hilt of his sword, as he so often did for comfort, only to be reminded that it wasn't there. Being with a lady with nothing but his bare hands to protect her in such a place had his heart racing.

The car pulled up to the hotel. Graham got their bags out of the trunk and followed Hannah to the entrance of this grand building.

The hotel's door went around in a circle, people walking in and out of it at the same time. He stopped and looked. He must have had a look on his face because Hannah took his arm with gentle encouragement.

"Just follow me." She smiled.

He took an uneasy step but followed her. Once inside, Hannah checked in. She spoke with people behind a large counter, while Graham looked around the lobby, trying to get his wits about him. Upon her return she gave him a room key.

"Here is your key. This way, to the elevator."

"What's this, then? This is not a key, this flat bit of plastic." He looked at her, aghast.

She smiled again. "Come on, I'll show you."

The feeling Graham couldn't get used to was feeling like he did not know how to protect this woman. He lived his life on high alert. From predators to Red Coats, something was always around. Graham could trust his gut to keep them safe in his own time, but in this time, he couldn't tell friend from foe.

He followed Hannah down the hallway until they came to two metal panels. He watched as Hannah pushed a little button on the wall that lit when she pushed it. A bell chimed as the doors slid open. Hannah walked in, and Graham peeked in.

"Come on, get in," she said as he reached for his hand.

He took it, and the spark that existed between them flickered.

Graham hesitantly crossed the line on the floor into a little compartment. He felt it shift beneath his weight. Hannah pushed the 8 button on the little wall, and the door slid close behind him. His heart raced. The floor lurched below him, and his stomach dropped. His chest tightened, and his heart pounded. He did not like the city, and he definitely did not like the moving box. He then felt Hannah's hand tighten around his. He was grateful for the anchor.

"Are you okay?" she asked.

Graham looked down at her. She smiled and rubbed gentle circles with her thumb on his hand. The spark grew with each small circle.

"This is an elevator. It is taking us up to the floor where our room is. You saw these in movies, remember."

Graham nodded.

Soon, the box stopped, which, again, caused his stomach to plummet, and the doors opened. He was glad to step out but was disappointed when Hannah took back her hand and headed down the hallway.

He followed her, and she stopped at a door. He watched as she took the little plastic card and slid it beneath the handle. The door whirred, a green light turned on, and she opened the door.

Hannah found a light and switched it on. Graham saw a room with a closet to one side and a bathroom on the other. When he walked in, he noticed big windows that overlooked the city, a table, a dresser with a large TV on it, and one very large bed featured prominently in the room. He looked around for another door leading to another bedroom, where Hannah would sleep.

"Oh, shoot, I forgot I made this reservation when I was supposed to be coming with Andy, let me call down and see if they have any other rooms available." She walked over to the table beside the bed and picked up the phone.

"Hi, I forgot to mention at check-in—is there any way we can switch to a room with two beds? Are you sure? It would be—no, I understand. Thanks anyway." She put the phone back in its cradle and turned to him.

"Well, looks like we are bunking together tonight," she said.

"What? Both of us in this room?"

"Both of us in this bed."

"No. That's not proper," he said, aghast.

"Proper or not, this is what we got. I promise to stay on my side."

"I canna sleep in that bed with ye," he protested.

The thought of sharing a bed with her thrilled and terrified him.

"Well, it is what it is. Sleep where you want," she said with a noticeable edge to her voice.

Surely, this isn't proper, and this cannot be what she wants, he thought. How were they to be expected to share a bed?

"Well, I most certainly am not sleeping in the same bed with ye, lass," he bit back, louder than he intended.

She looked away from him but not before he noted an expression he didn't quite recognize. The fire was all but gone from her right then, and Graham feared that expression might be hurt.

"I'm sorry . . . I understand you do not want to share a bed with me . . . , but it is what it is. Let's just get ready for the ceremony," she said, sounding defeated.

Graham kicked himself for losing his temper. It was just so easy to do when everything was off. He didn't want to sleep in the same bed with her because it wasn't proper, not because he didn't want to. Spending a night snuggled up against those soft curves was something he thought about more than he would have liked to admit. And his thoughts were not only improper—they were downright indecent.

After a while, Graham slipped into his suit. He had not yet become accustomed to modern pants. He much preferred the roominess of his kilt. He was dressed except for the tie. No way could he remember how to tie that thing properly. He would have to wait for Hannah to help him, which he despised. Though Hannah did seem accustomed to helping people, he did not want to be another task for Hannah. He didn't see any way around it, to his own frustration—yet another reason he despised the tie in his hand.

Hannah had been in the bathroom for quite some time. The shower water had been off for a while, where the whirring became prominent, then quiet. He wondered what she was up to.

A while later, the bathroom door opened. The sight of her nearly took his breath away and made all the blood rush to places it had no business going. He fought the urge to adjust his pants. She was wearing an emerald-green dress that hugged her in all the right places and plunged deep to reveal her cleavage. Her hair was curled with blonde bouncy waves. As she walked over to Graham, the aroma of roses and freshness hit him. She turned her back to him, and Graham saw the way the dress hugged her ass.

He saw the pale soft skin of her back. And he was definitely indecent if she had looked at him right then. She lifted her hair and revealed a smattering of freckles across her shoulders.

"Could you zip me up?" she asked.

"Oh . . . of course."

He reached forward, grabbed the little zipper, and pulled. His fingers brushed the impossibly smooth skin of her back. He wanted to kiss her neck and nuzzle her and breathe in her scent. Then he wanted to throw her down on the huge bed and rumple her pretty little dress and claim her. He had been fighting this feeling for a while, but right then, it seemed almost impossible to fight.

She turned. Their faces inches apart.

"Thank you," she said breathlessly, her cheeks flushed.

"Do you need help?"

Could she see the straining against his trousers? Was she offering to help him with his arousal? Surely, that was improper.

"Help." He swallowed. "Help with what?"

"Your tie."

She pulled the silk tie he had draped around his neck. She lifted the collar. The closeness to her drove him mad. All he would have to do was lean forward a mere couple of inches to claim her mouth and wrap his arms around her and hold her soft curves against his taut body.

She tied an impeccable knot and pulled it up around his neck. He fought the urge because he was not a scoundrel, and Hannah deserved to be treated like a queen, not quickly bedded like a common whore. Although, part of him secretly hoped those expectations were different in modern times, too. Maybe modern women would have liked to be treated both ways?

He took a deep breath and turned from Hannah as soon

as she had finished fixing his collar. He needed to get himself under control. He took a long drink of water.

Hannah looked herself over in the full-length mirror outside the bathroom door. Smiling, she huffed and quirked her head.

"This will do," she said with a shrug.

"You look beautiful," Graham said once he had gotten himself under control.

"You clean up pretty nice yourself," she said, looking him over. "Do you want to go down to the bar and get a drink before the ceremony starts?"

She handed him her phone and the little plastic key card and asked him to put them in his pocket before walking down to the bar.

They were finishing up dinner at the reception. Graham noticed the reception was different from his time but not entirely. The dinner itself was similar to a feast, different but enough similarities that he felt confident in his own actions. They were sitting with some of Hannah's former coworkers. They kept asking her about where she was going next and what her next career move was. She was on top of the question, talking about taking time off, maybe doing some traveling.

"Well, you can always go work for your dad if you can't find another job," said one of the men sitting at the table with an air of smugness.

"That is an option, but I don't need handouts from my family to get a good job," Hannah said.

The man scooted his chair back and glared at Hannah.

"Come on, let's go get a drink," he said to the woman next to him. They both left the table.

"Damn, Hannah," said one of the other guys at the table, sounding impressed.

"What? We all know the only reason he was promoted

was that he married the boss's daughter. I don't work there anymore. Why do I need to let him be a dick?" she said. She seemed to be pretty pleased with herself.

Graham was pleased with her, too. He loved that fire back in her eyes. He loved how strong she was, even when he was on the receiving end. It lit something in him. She could decimate anyone at this table with her words, yet sometimes, she seemed to shrink away, and the fire would go out. She was still a puzzle he was piecing together.

The DJ started playing music. He wasn't sure he would classify some of it as music, and the dancing was like nothing Graham had seen. Although, the slower songs seemed to be easy enough to dance to. Graham looked over to see the bride walking over to the table. She sat at the empty chair next to Hannah.

"Hannah, I miss you around the office," she said as she gave her a hug.

"Aww, I miss you, too, Sadie. You look absolutely stunning."

"Oh, this old thing?" she said with a smile. "When you're back in the city, we have to do lunch."

"Yeah, that sounds good."

Sadie turned to Graham. "Make sure you get her out on the dance floor, she's got moves."

Graham smiled at Hannah. "You've got 'moves'? Well, I'd love to see them."

"Your accent. Are you Scottish?"

"Aye," Graham answered with a smile.

"Where are you from? I spent a semester in Edinburgh," she said.

"I'm from Glencoe."

"That's some beautiful area over there?"

"Aye, 'tis."

"Hey, Hannah, hot and an accent. Your life is really coming together after leaving the firm."

Hannah blushed and smiled. "Don't you have guests to attend to?"

"Right," she said, hugging Hannah one last time. "It was really good to see you." She turned to Graham. "And I was serious about getting her out on the dance floor."

Graham nodded and smiled.

The music turned from a faster pace to a slow song. Graham had seen how these were done. He wanted to hold her close, if only for a song. So, he pushed back his chair and stood.

"What do ye say? Hannah Glenn, would ye do me the honor of dancing with me?"

"You don't have to do this," she said.

"Please dance with me. Dinna make me beg ye?"

Hannah smiled. She tried to seem put off, but he could tell she was pleased.

Graham led her to the dance floor, took her hand, placed the other on the small of her back, and pulled her close. It would be downright indecent in his time, but he wasn't complaining. The intoxicating aroma of her perfume still hung in the air between them. The dance seemed to lighten Hannah a bit. After some of the dinner conversation, she seemed a little worried.

When that song ended, a faster one came on.

"I love this song!" she said, still holding Graham's hand.

"Oh, a song, that's what this is?"

"Yep, this is a song. Now dance with me."

"I dinna think I can dance to this. It just sounds like noise to me."

"Just watch. It's easy. Just move to the beat," she said. She moved her hips back and forth. As long as he got to watch her move like that, he would do his best to figure out how to keep up. Watching her shake and shimmy her shoulders had Graham in a state.

She sang along to the words and smiled, her hips swaying.

Though this was nothing like what Graham was accustomed to, he caught on and attempted to keep up. He danced with Hannah for the next couple of songs.

"How is yer ankle?" he asked after their last slow dance.

"What?" she said to him.

He leaned closer and said, "Yer ankle, those shoes look like they would be easy to injure yerself on the spikes with yer weak ankle."

"Oh, it's doing okay. Do you want to take a break and get some drinks?"

"Aye, you go sit down, and I'll get us some wine."

Graham headed to the bar, enjoying himself. Though the music was different, the celebration seemed familiar, and it didn't hurt that he was with the bonniest girl in the room.

Graham stopped by the restroom. He bumped into the man who had been so rude at dinner. He was talking with another man with the same air of rich-boy entitlement Graham could recognize in any century.

"Did you see her out there on the dance floor? It's embarrassing," said the guy from the table.

"You're just pissed because she called you out for having a job at your father-in-law's firm," the other guy joked.

Graham realized they were talking about Hannah.

"Whatever. She's a bitch. Why's she even here?"

Graham's blood was boiling. He tapped the man's shoulder, who turned and was clearly drunk.

"Oh, it's this guy!" He put his arm around Graham and showed him to his friend. "This guy is her date."

"Let me ask you. What's is like being with her? She must be a good fuck to put up with her attitude. That bitch needs to learn her place," he said, slurring, patting Graham on the chest.

That was it.

Graham stepped back, raised his fist, and punched the man square in the jaw. He fell to the floor.

Laid out on the ground, looking dazed, he rubbed his jaw as his friend helped him up.

"What the fuck, Graham?!"

He heard a familiar voice behind him. He turned to see Hannah standing behind him fuming. She turned on her heel and walked down the hallway.

"Aww, Christ, Hannah, wait." He followed her as she booked it down the hallway. "Hannah, stop. That guy had it comin'. He was a drunken arse, and I dinna even hit him that hard."

Hannah stopped and whipped around.

"I know he is a dick, but there are ways of behaving, of dealing with guys like that. You just can't haul off and punch people." She turned again and headed to the box.

Graham caught up to her as she repeatedly stabbed at the up arrow.

"Hannah, I'm sorry if I've done anything wrong, but I'll not be sorry for striking him. After what he said, he's lucky that's all I did."

Hannah squared off to him, fire blazing in her eyes. "Yeah, I know that toxic male bullshit. Can't deal with some emotions and just fly off the handle and punch people and make it worse."

Graham looked her in the eyes, passions of all kinds flowing through him. "I dinna ken what toxic male bullshit is, but there are some things that a man deserved to get a beatin' for, and talkin' the way he did is one of them. Think I'm a brute all ye want. He had it comin'."

The doors opened. They stood back and politely smiled

as an older couple stepped out of the doors. They got in, and Hannah pushed the button before turning to him again and poked an angry finger into his chest.

"Maybe he did, but did you stop and think about the repercussions of that decision? You just punched my old boss's son-in-law at a wedding, with many prominent members of law firms here. How does that look for me? I have to be perfect. I work twice as hard to get half as far because of the way I look. Now, not only am I fat, but I also have a neanderthal boyfriend who goes around punching people. Not that you are my boyfriend, but that is the way it will be perceived. Did you even think about me?"

The doors opened, and she was halfway down the hallway, leaving Graham to figure out what had just happened.

"Now just wait a bloody moment!" he called. He caught up with her at the room door while she fiddled with the key. "Since when do ye care about what people think about ye? I didn't think ye wanted to be a lawyer anyway, and I was thinking about ye. He said some unspeakable things. Hannah, don't ye see I am always thinking about ye. Now, I'm sorry if I complicated things for ye, if ye still want to work there, but I will not be sorry for punching someone who needed to be punched."

By the time he got all of that out, Hannah was already in the room.

She stopped, turned around, and looked at him. "You think about me?" She looked stunned. Her chest was heaving, her cheeks flushed.

"Yes, for the love of God, woman, you are all I think about," he said as the door shut behind him.

"I am?" she said breathlessly. Her full lips parted, and she looked up at him.

The look on her face. The surprise from his confession.

How could she not know? She drove him mad in every sense of the word.

He took a step toward her and grabbed her shoulders. He bent his head down and laid claim to her mouth—the mouth he had wanted to taste for so long—and kissed her.

She pushed him away and stepped back.

"I'm sorry," he said. "I shouldn't have done that." He stepped away from her.

Hannah grabbed him by the hand and stepped close. She then reached up, grabbed his face, and kissed him. Hard. He wrapped his arms around her waist and held her close to him, returning the kiss. She got her hand into his long red hair and pressed herself into him. He felt the softness of all her curves pressed into the hardness of his own body.

He stopped. She groaned at the absence of his mouth.

"Hannah, I dinna want ye to do anything ye dinna want to do. I dinna ken all the rules of courting in this day and age."

"Shut up and kiss me."

That was all he needed.

He grabbed her and pulled her back into a kiss. His hand sank into the ample curves of her ass. Her mouth opened, and he claimed her mouth. Her tongue danced with his, and Graham sucked on it. He had wanted it for so long.

An abrupt knock on the door shattered that moment. They both stopped and looked at each other, flushed and dazed.

"Hannah . . . are you in there?" a voice called from the other side.

Hannah froze. Graham looked down at her, her face riddled with an expression he didn't quite know how to read.

"Hannah. It's Andy. I ran into Sadie downstairs . . . Ya know, at her wedding—I was supposed to be your date, I'm not mad. I just wanna talk."

Graham looked down at Hannah. She was still in his embrace. She pushed away and walked to the door.

"Who the devil is Andy?" Graham asked, his eyes boring into Hannah.

"He's my ex-boyfriend," Hannah whispered back at him harshly.

Graham felt his anger rising.

"Why is he here?" Graham demanded.

"I have no idea," Hannah spat back.

"Han, come on, can I come in? I hear you in there. Can we just talk? You won't answer any of my texts or phone calls," he said.

Hannah walked over to the door and cracked it. She peeked her head into the hallway and said, "That is because we broke up, Andy."

Graham stepped behind her and pulled the door open, revealing himself, towering behind her. "Can I help ye?" he said to Andy, his voice low and menacing.

Andy looked up at him. His eyes widened. *That's right*, Graham thought. *Run away, scared little boy*. He made a fist at his side, and his knuckles popped.

Andy's chest filled with a fake bravado that barely covered his fear.

"Who's this?" he said.

"I am her date tonight," Graham said. He would not strike anyone else that night, but emotions were running high.

"Oh my god! You"—she put her hand on Graham's chest —"take a breath. I will be right back."

"You," she said, pointing at Andy, "let's talk."

She stepped out into the hall and closed the door behind her.

Graham felt all the emotions inside of him boiling up. From the guy at the bar to the guy at the door to that kiss. *That kiss!*

"Aargh!" Graham bellowed in the empty room trying to get rid of some of the rage inside of him. If only they were at the farmhouse, he could take a walk. Being in a tiny room in a city he didn't know in an unfamiliar time, he felt like a caged animal.

CHAPTER 10

"*A*ndy! What the fuck are you doing here?" Hannah asked.

"You won't answer my phone calls. I have been going nuts without you," he said.

Graham yelled, his voice carrying into the hallway.

"Hannah, I can't leave you here with him. He's not safe. I heard he punched someone. It's all they are talking about at the wedding downstairs."

"A wedding you should not even be at. We broke up, Andy. Done. Clean break, and I assure you, I am perfectly safe in that room. You, on the other hand, might not be."

The bathroom door slammed.

"Let's walk and talk." Hannah felt the need to put some space between Andy and Graham. Emotions were high.

They found a generic lounge area next to the ice machine, and Hannah stopped.

"Talk, Andy. What is it you need to say?"

"Babe, I fucked up. I should not have been chillin' at your apartment without you. I just miss you, and I want you back," he said, reaching for Hannah's hand.

Hannah batted his hand away.

"If this is about the guy in your hotel room, I don't care about that. I don't care what has happened since we've been on a break. I just wanna make it better."

"Andy. No. I was not happy in our relationship. You never once planned a date. You never once paid for dinner. You never once made any effort. Even on my birthday and Valentine's Day. I am worth the effort, Andy. I realize that now. I meant it. We are done."

"So, what, you are just with that red-headed rage monster now?"

"Number one, we are not dating, but I would be lucky to have him. He has taken better care of me in a month than you ever did in the year we were together. No, he shouldn't have hit anyone, but he was trying to stick up for me. Number two, you don't get a say in my life. Period."

Then Andy collapsed onto the bench and cried. Hannah could not believe he was crying.

"Andy . . ." She sat next to him.

He turned and put his head on her shoulder. She awkwardly patted him on the back, unsure of what to do. She had never been on this end of things before.

"I know I screwed up, Hannah. I'm sorry. I just don't know what to do. My whole life is a mess without you. I got a job, but it's only part-time, and now Carlos and his girlfriend are getting married, and I know they are going to want me to move out. Where else am I going to find a place to live . . . ?" He sniffled. "Sadie may have mentioned that you have been staying at your parent's farmhouse . . . so, you just have that apartment sitting, empty. Could I maybe just move in until I figure my stuff out?"

"There it is," Hannah said, pushing his head off her shoulder to stand. "That's what this is all about."

"What? Hannah, no," he said quickly.

"Andy . . . look at me. Look in my eyes. You are not my problem anymore. We are over. I mean that, and I'm not going to change my mind. You cannot live in my apartment. If you get kicked out, go home to New Jersey. You know your mom will let you move in. Now, if you excuse me, I need to go." She turned on her heel and propelled toward her room.

Hannah wasn't sure what she was walking back into. She had been in the middle of what was probably the hottest kiss of her entire life, only for her ex-boyfriend to interrupt it. Graham had to be fuming. Hannah stopped outside of her door.

She didn't know what to do or even what she wanted. She was confused. She didn't want to face Graham. She was mad at him for being a brute, but she also wanted to rip all of his clothes off and ride him, feelings she wasn't used to, definitely not a part of her five-year plan, that's for sure. But that plan was out the window ever since she had quit her job; she was just flying by the seat of her pants. It was terrifying and exhilarating, but right then, she was disoriented and didn't know how to feel.

She took a deep breath and opened the door.

When she opened the door, she heard running water. Graham was in the shower. Hannah changed into her pajamas and got into bed.

He was in the shower for a very long time. When she heard the water cut off, she closed her eyes and pretended to sleep. Sure, it may not have been the most mature thing she had ever done, but it would buy her some time. The bathroom door opened, and the smell of his shampoo filled the room. She heard him walk over to her.

"Hannah," he whispered. He put his hand lightly on her shoulder.

She didn't stir. He pulled the blanket up over her shoulders and sat in the chair across the room.

THE NEXT MORNING, Hannah woke up and looked for Graham. He was sleeping in the chair next to the bed, his feet kicked up on the table. He had his head resting on a pillow against the wall. He looked uncomfortable. She couldn't believe he had slept like that all night and left her a huge bed.

Her mind was still reeling from the night before, that kiss replaying in her head as she wondered what could have happened if stupid Andy hadn't ruined everything. But on the other hand, was that even something she wanted? She wanted it, but was it a good idea, with him leaving in a few short months?

She got out of the bed swiftly and tip-toed into the bathroom.

"Hannah," she whispered to herself in the mirror, "pull it together." She washed her face, brushed her teeth, and got dressed. She hoped they could get out of there before running into anyone from the wedding. Get them back to the safety of the farmhouse and figure it out.

She left the bathroom and packed. Graham was already awake, sitting in the chair, wiping the sleep from his eyes.

"Good morning," he said, smiling at her.

"Good morning," Hannah said, breaking eye contact. "I think we should get out of here early so we don't run into anyone from the wedding last night."

"Oh . . . right," Graham said.

She could tell he was trying to make sense of what was going on.

"Hannah, about last night—"

"Let's just get packed up."

"As ye wish," he said and went into the bathroom.

Hannah sat on the edge of the bed and tried to catch her breath. She wasn't used to this. She felt out of control. In the past, she had been trapped by bad boyfriends and a job she hated. But now, she was trying to build the life she wanted, and she was scared.

If you fail at something you hate, then who cares? If you lose the love of someone you never really loved anyway, good on to the next person. This didn't feel like that. This felt new. Hannah could feel herself closing off. If she failed going after her dream, then that is a failure she wasn't sure she could come back from.

So, she stood, gathered all the items in the room, and waited for Graham.

CHAPTER 11

*U*neasy silence filled the train ride. Graham loaded the suitcases into the back of Hannah's car, and they headed back to the farmhouse.

His head was still spinning from the previous night. He had been an arse, but he couldn't help it. He was so angry at the man for talking the way he did. And that kiss. He had kissed a few lasses in his day, but it was never anything like that. He hoped maybe things would change in his relationship with Hannah. But then, when her ex showed up at the door, it took all of Graham's power not to shut the door in his face and carry Hannah off to bed.

If she didn't want that—or even worse, regretted what had happened the night before—he would let it go, but he knew his heart was spoken for, in that timeline and even his own. He had never known a woman with such fire.

He longed for that fire, but all he got was ice. He wasn't sure how to proceed. They only spoke when necessary the whole journey home. It felt wrong, but he had to try to make it right.

The car pulled up to the farmhouse, and Graham brought bags inside.

Once they were in the kitchen, he said, "Hannah, can we talk for a moment?"

"Thanks for bringing the bags in. Just leave them there. I'll take care of it," she said, not meeting his eye.

"Hannah—"

"Sam was here to take care of the horses this morning. You might want to go check on them."

"Hannah," he said a bit more firmly. "The horses can wait."

She finally met his eye and took a breath.

Graham could swear he saw her bottom lip quiver as she turned to head up the stairs.

"Hannah Glenn, will ye please speak to me? What did I do? Did I hurt ye? Are ye still cross about that man at the wedding? I would take it back if I could. Please, I'm going mad over here."

She looked at him and shook her head. "You didn't hurt me."

"Well, I'm glad of that, at least. If ye dinna want me that's fine. I just wanted to make sure ye were well." He looked at her, his face earnest.

"Graham . . . I'm sorry. After last night I . . . I feel out of control. I am bad at feeling out of control."

"I would never force ye to do anything ye dinna want to do," he reassured her. Taking a step forward, he wanted to comfort her.

"I know that."

"Good . . ." he said, looking her in the eye.

He was glad of that at least, but he still wanted more of this woman.

"Now I know times are different, and I'm not certain how

to go about courting ye. Most of the time, in my day, marriages were arranged, but there were some love marriages, and they started differently." Her eyes got big, and he panicked. "I'm not saying I wanna marry ye . . . I don't know what I'm saying." He made a low guttural sound and a string of Gaelic words. "All I know is I like being around ye. I very much liked kissin' ye last night, and yer drivin' me mad, woman."

A warm smile crept across her face.

"I don't know about marriage, but how about a date?"

"I dinna ken what a date is, but if I get to be with ye, then, yes."

"And don't call me woman," she said, giving him a sly smile.

"But ye are a woman, and a bonny one at that."

Hannah looked down, and Graham noticed her cheeks flush.

She took a breath and bit her bottom lip.

This woman was going to be the death of him. He wanted to take care of her and do unspeakable things with her. He wanted everything.

"Okay, well, I'm going to go take a shower, and you should go check on the horses, but meet me back up here for dinner. We will go on a proper date."

"Aye, I would like that very much."

"Okay, well, I'm going to go get the city washed off me, but I will see you soon." She turned and started up the stairs. She made it up a couple, then she turned around and looked at him, her bottom lip between her teeth. "For our date."

"Aye, for our date," he said with a reassuring nod.

As he entered the stable, he tried to think of all the movies Hannah had shown him. He had been watching for history and a general understanding of the present day, but some of them definitely showed modern courtship.

He needed some time to get his head back on straight. He

needed to prove to her that he was not some big brute who would strike every man that made him angry, that he could control his temper and treat her how modern women deserved to be treated. He wanted to lighten the burden she seemed to constantly be carrying. Hannah deserved all of that and more. In his short time there, he had grown very fond of her.

So, he would take that moment, think back to the movies they had watched together, and figure out the proper etiquette for a date.

CHAPTER 12

*H*annah stepped out on the porch just in time to see Graham leaving the stables. He had on boots, jeans that were just tight enough, a plain black T-shirt, and a jacket over it. His hair was down, and the sunset made it look almost like fire. He took Hannah's breath away. He did not look like he belonged, but in the same breath, Hannah felt like he was home. Like, somehow, he did belong there with her. Those were dangerous thoughts about a man who would be gone in five months.

Hannah wanted to treat this like a date, like a real date. She had curled her hair and done her makeup, which wasn't something she had done often. She also put on her favorite blue sweater that hugged her curves and made her cleavage look out of this world. She still wasn't sure what she wanted, but she wouldn't mind another mind-blowing kiss with Graham. Even though that might complicate her already too complicated feelings.

Graham walked up to the porch and held out his hand to help Hannah down the stairs. "My lady," he said as he walked her to the car. "You look radiant."

Hannah felt her cheeks flush.

"Thank you. Do you like Italian food?"

"Italian food? Never been. France was as far as I ever got."

"Right . . . well, we aren't going to Italy, just a restaurant."

"Aye," he said as he opened her car door and helped her in.

Hannah was trying to adjust to his chivalry. She liked it, but she was not used to that kind of treatment. In her relationships in the past, she would wear the pants, making the decisions. The guys she dated weren't the chivalrous type; they were more of the infantile type. It was an adjustment to the treatment she wasn't entirely certain she deserved.

They went to eat at a little Italian bistro in town. They sat at a tiny table in the corner, complete with a candle burning in the middle and a red-and-white checkered tablecloth. The waitress stopped by, took their orders, and opened a bottle of wine for them to share.

They both ordered a plate of spaghetti. Hannah couldn't help but smile, watching Graham trying to eat the long noodles for the first time. He got sauce all over his chin and shirt. He made a guttural noise and muttered in Gaelic as he tried for another bite.

Hannah chuckled.

"Glad this amuses ye," he said, looking up at her.

"Here, do this." She showed him how to twirl the pasta onto his fork.

She watched as he figured it out. He stopped for a drink of wine and caught Hannah admiring him. A soft smile settled on his face. She reached across the table and wiped a spot of sauce from his chin. He caught her hand and pressed a small kiss to it. They sat there, her hand in his on the table, his thumb grazing her knuckles. She melted into a puddle and clenched her thighs.

Their hands clasped, and with the candle burning, they

talked, sharing more of their personal stories than they ever had before.

"So, you've met my crazy family. Tell me about yours?" asked Hannah.

"What would ye like to know?"

"Anything. Do you have siblings? What are your parents like?"

"I had two brothers, an older brother, and a younger brother. I also had a younger sister. When I was twelve, she and my mother fell ill and died. So, it was just us men for a long time. My younger brother, and I went to fight in France. He didn't make it back." He paused and took a drink of wine. "He died on the battlefield. When I came back to Scotland, my elder brother had been killed by a British soldier who was trying to take a horse from our stable. My father was arrested shortly after and was hung as a traitor to the crown for treason. That is why I joined the cause and came to stay with my uncle."

"Wow, I had no idea. I'm so sorry."

"I don't need yer pity. 'Tis a sad tale, but many other of my countrymen have similar tales. It was a much harsher time than now, I am learning. I am grateful ye have not had to experience such tragedy. Ye asked about my family. There it is. But I spent my time as a wee lad in a loud, happy family for the most part. I choose to remember those times."

"Do you miss home?"

"Aye," he said. He bit his lip and slowly nodded his head. "It has been an adjustment to living here. Scotland is a beautiful land, and the stark contrast to the city we were in yesterday did make me a bit homesick. I could not live there. It is too loud, and there is no green, anyway. It is better here. The hills and valleys remind me of home, but it is still hard to feel out of place. To never really know how to behave and not be able to take care of myself—it has been frustrating."

"I think I forget that sometimes. I will try to remember how hard this must be for you. But if it makes you feel any better, I know plenty of men who are way less capable than you and have lived in this time their whole life."

"Well, I'm not certain if I should find that comforting or disappointing at the quality of men in yer life, but I appreciate it nonetheless." Squeezing her hand, he gaver her a reassuring smile.

Hannah felt like she had just been let in on a secret. She saw his humanity and not as a magical creature. He had a past and tragedy. On some level, she had always known that, but it grounded him to her reality even more.

"I apologize if that was a bit of a heavy topic for a date," he said.

"No," she reassured. "I asked. I'm glad you told me. I feel like I know you more."

He brought her hand up to his lips and kissed it.

The candle burning in the glass bottle had dripped down to almost nothing. Hannah looked around, and the restaurant had emptied.

"Should we head back?" she asked.

Graham nodded. He got up and gave Hannah a hand to help her up. As they walked back to the car, Hannah laced her arm through Graham's. It felt natural to walk with him like that. Like it was how it always should have been.

When they arrived back at the house, Graham walked Hannah up to the door.

"I believe it is customary to have a goodnight kiss after a date."

"Oh, you've been doing your research," Hannah said, smiling.

"I just want to make sure I am doing this in the correct manner. Ye deserve to be treated like a lady . . . ye know for your own time," he said as he rested his hand on her upper arm. "So, . . . may I kiss ye?"

Hannah nodded at him, and her heart skipped a beat. She felt a flutter she had never felt before.

He cupped her face with one of his large rough hands and brought his face down to hers, sliding his other hand around her waist, pulling her in close to him. He kissed her with such gentleness Hannah felt her heart break and rearrange.

They had shared a kiss the previous night. That kiss had been a build up of passion and pure attraction and fire. This kiss felt like fondness. This kiss was reverent. This kiss felt like she was precious to him. Hannah didn't know how to respond to this kiss. Her breath shuddered, and she could feel Graham about to pull away, which might have killed her, so she leaned into the kiss, pressing into him. He held her a bit more tightly and slid the hand that had been resting on her jaw up into her hair. He parted her mouth, and their tongues found each other. Both melted into this kiss.

Something was happening. Something important. Hannah could feel it, and it scared her, but right then, all she wanted to do was keep kissing him. But then he stopped.

He gave her one last quick gentle kiss and said, "Good night, Hannah Glenn."

She was a little breathless and disoriented from the absence of his mouth.

"Did you want to come in for a little bit?" Hannah asked, not ready for this to end.

"No, I think I better head back to the stable for the night?"

Hannah felt like the balloon that had been filling inside her with that kiss was just let go, and the air was rushing out and flying everywhere.

"Oh, right . . . yeah . . . that's good . . . well, good night." She turned to go inside.

Graham stopped her and grabbed her hand. "What just happened?"

"What do you mean?" she asked, trying to be as nonchalant as possible.

"Hannah, I can't be the only one who felt something in that kiss. Why did ye react in such a way just now?"

"I'm sorry. I invited you in, and you declined, so I thought—"

"I declined because I am trying to do this right. I want to treat ye like ye deserve to be treated. I want ye to trust me and maybe even like me, not bed me because ye can't decide if ye want to throw me out the window or into yer bed. Just so ye know . . . I'll always prefer a bed, especially with you," he said with a wink. "I just want to show ye more."

"Oh . . . okay." Hannah looked to the ground and bit her lip. His hand found her face again and turned it to his, so he could look into her eyes.

"So, good night Hannah, I will see ye tomorrow."

Hannah felt the little glow inside her return, the little spark of possibility.

She bit her lip and looked up at him. He looked back at her with a kindness she hadn't fully seen before.

"Good night," she said with a small smile.

She turned to go back into the house. After she closed the door, she pressed her back up against it. The small smile grew and grew until it was all over her face and all she could feel. She was giddy. She hadn't felt truly giddy in a very long time. Hannah had learned to not get her hopes up when it came to most men. She didn't allow men to make her feel like this. She used to think the men who caused these feelings were out of her league, which is why she settled for guys like Andy. Graham was not that kind of guy. She relaxed into the feeling, pushing aside all the complications.

CHAPTER 13

*O*ver the next couple of days, Hannah and Graham spent time together. Hannah would bring him breakfast, and they would ride horses or take a walk in the woods. Hannah found time to work on writing, while Graham busied himself with projects around the barn and had started to help Sam with some projects next door. They would come back together for dinner and share their days and stories. They would steal kisses—nice, sweet kisses during the day and longer, passionate kisses at night. Hannah very much wanted to rip his clothes off, but she respected his wishes to learn more about each other first.

That morning, Hannah was up getting coffee ready and making breakfast. She heard the door open and turned to see Graham heading inside.

"Good morning," she said to him as she turned to flip a pancake.

Graham snuck in behind her, put his arms around her waist, and whispered, "Good morning, mo ghrádh (*mo-ghry*)."

He had taken to calling Hannah that sometime over the last couple of days. She hadn't asked yet what it meant, but she liked the sound of it coming out of his mouth.

"Did you sleep okay?" she asked.

"Like a log . . . I just want to tell ye dinna make dinner plans tonight."

Hannah took the last pancake off the griddle and turned to look at him with one eyebrow raised. "Okay?"

Graham grinned at her and snatched a piece of bacon.

"What do you have planned?"

"Oh, well, now ye ken I canna tell ye that."

"I don't like surprises."

"Well, I hate to see ye suffer, but yer just going to have to be patient." He grinned at her.

"I suck at patience."

"That, I ken, and I like to keep ye on yer toes," he said, giving her a little kiss. "I am going over to help Sam after I get the horses out to pasture. Be ready for dinner. Dress for the outdoors."

"Okay . . ." Hannah eyed him suspiciously as he ate pancakes.

He merely smiled at her and waggled his eyebrows.

"You are really going to make me wait all day and just tell me to dress for the outdoors," she said as she sat down with her plate of pancakes and mug of coffee.

"I am," he said, grinning from ear to ear.

Hannah pretended to look at him disapprovingly, but she was excited. None of her previous boyfriends had even planned a date, much less whatever Graham was planning.

Graham took his dishes to the sink, rinsed them, put them in the dishwasher, and turned back to her.

"I will see you this evening." He walked over, gave her a quick kiss, and headed out the door.

For the rest of the day, Hannah busied herself around the house and with her writing. She texted Poppy and tried to pass the time.

Finally, the time came. Hannah sat on the porch in boots, leggings, a sweater, and a jean jacket over it. She saw Graham coming from the stables. She walked down to meet him.

"Are ye ready?" he asked her.

"Ready as I'll ever be," she answered. "Lead the way."

He took her by the hand, and they walked to one of the trails. She noticed he was carrying two bags.

"What's in the bags?" she asked.

"Patience, mo ghrádh."

They walked down the path in the woods by the creek. They came to a little clearing, and Hannah saw a blanket laid out with pillows, a string of fairy lights strung in the trees, and a fire going. He pulled out a bottle of wine and two wine glasses along with a wooden cutting board and some little containers filled with various cheeses, fruits, and meats.

"Wow, Graham, you did all of this?"

"Well, Jackson helped a bit. He said ye would like this sharutry . . . sharcurky . . . Och. Its food cut up into wee bites," he said, shaking his head.

"Charcuterie." She smiled at him. "This is really incredible. No one has ever gone to this much trouble for me before."

"Well, that is a shame. You deserve this and so much more."

They ate their dinner as the sun set.

Graham retrieved something else from his bag.

"I remember making these with you and your family that first night. I thought ye might like some."

"S'mores! Yes!"

So, they sat on the blanket, roasting s'mores.

Hannah sat, bracketed by Graham's legs, her back against his strong chest, her head resting on his shoulder. Silently, they looked up at the stars. Hannah held one of his big hands in hers, lightly tracing the calluses on his hand. He shifted over and sighed.

"How is it that ye always smell so good?" he whispered.

Hannah could feel his breath, and his mouth made the tiniest accidental contact with her ear, turning her into a puddle right there on the spot. Just being around him unraveled her. She turned and tipped her head to look at him.

He was perfect. Fuck. Hannah was a goner. She could not remember ever feeling like this before.

"Can I ask ye a question?"

"Anything."

"I am still trying to figure out the proper ways of courting in your time. I very much liked the kiss in the hotel, and I would very much like to kiss you like that again, but I worry about being improper."

She tried to sit up to turn to face him, but he held her to him.

"I know ye hate when I talk about things being improper, but just hear me out."

She relaxed back into him.

"I canna help but notice that things are different here. I would very much like to be a modern boyfriend to ye, but I dinna ken how. In my day, I would have married ye long ago, and there would have been no choice in the matter after a kiss like that in the hotel and the lust in my heart."

She felt more than the lust in his heart; Hannah could also feel the lust in his pants pressing into her back.

"I've never felt that much desire and passion in my life. I just dinna want to behave in such a way that would make ye uncomfortable or go too far."

Hannah sat up and turned to face him. "Graham, do you trust me?"

"What do ye mean?"

"Do you trust me?" she asked again.

"Of course, I do."

"Then, please trust that I will not do anything I don't want to do. I assure you that I can take care of myself."

"Of that, I have no doubt. You are one of the most capable women I have ever met. I very much would like to kiss you."

"What are you waiting for?"

He leaned forward and kissed her. At first, it was slow and sweet but then Hannah took his bottom lip into her mouth and bit. He groaned as she sucked it. Graham's hand fisted her hair and pulled to deepen the kiss.

Hannah pulled away, panting a bit. Then she adjusted herself to straddle his legs. She looked at him. His eyes were hooded, burning with passion. Hannah hadn't seen this look since that truly magical kiss in the hotel. The spark that existed between them was starting to engulf her.

She crashed into him, taking his mouth. Her hands slid from his chest up over his shoulders and into his hair. He started kissing down her neck. Hannah took off her jacket. She was on fire.

Graham kissed her collar bone, and his hands found her ass. He pulled her into him, and she could feel his erection press between her legs. They were still fully dressed, but that sensation sent sparks flying inside of her. She cried out.

Graham pulled back and looked at her, assessing what her noises meant. When he was certain it was a cry of pleasure, he went back to kissing her. His hands explored her body. He ran his hands up her back, holding her close as he trailed down her chest. His mouth and his hands ventured closer to her breasts but never close enough. Her nipples pebbled under her sweater, screaming for attention. She did what needed to be done.

She pulled out of his grasp, let her hands find the hem of her sweater, and pulled it over her head. Graham growled, brought his hand up, cupped her breast outside of her lacy bra.

"Christ, Hannah, you are beautiful."

He claimed her mouth again, his hands exploring her breasts. He pinched her nipple, and Hannah cried out. In one swift move, he flipped her on her back, and he was there, between her legs. He ground into her and kissed her.

He kissed her neck and shoulder. Then he yanked the cup of her bra and freed her breast. He took it into his mouth and sucked. Hannah saw stars. He was grinding his cock into her thin leggings. She could feel the seam of his jeans, desperately wishing he had fewer clothes on. He swirled his tongue around her nipple as his other hand found her hips and pulled her even closer. Hannah thought she might have an orgasm right there. That was unheard of for her. She was panting.

"Graham, take your shirt off. I want to feel your skin against mine."

He immediately obeyed. He was going back for her nipple, but Hannah reached up and stopped him. He looked at her. His pupils were blown as he panted, ready to devour her.

"You're so fucking hot," she said, running her hands over his chest.

There were a few sparse red hairs, and he was hard with muscles. He bent back down and kissed her. Hannah was only slightly aware of the thunder rumbling in the distance.

She ran his hands up and down his back as he ground into her. His mouth and hands seemed to be everywhere at once. This was by far the hottest moment of Hannah's life.

She was on fire. She was going to come. She was going to come right there, in that clearing, with her pants on. She was going to come from his grinding between her legs, his mouth on her nipples, his hand on her ass.

She felt something on her face. She didn't register what it was until there was a loud crash of thunder. At that moment, the skies opened, and it started pouring. Neither of them stopped. With the second loud crash of thunder, Graham pulled himself up.

"We should go," he said.

He sat up to a kneeling position between Hannah's legs. Hannah groaned.

"Come on, mo ghrádh, let's get ye home before it picks up."

He handed Hannah her sweater. He put his shirt on and started packing up. Hannah put on her sweater. By the time she was done, he had everything packed up. He held his hand out as she got up from the blanket, then picked it up.

"Let's go."

He took her by the hand, and they ran back to the house. He ran at a slow pace, remembering Hannah could not run as fast, guiding her down the dark trail and helping her swiftly over the creek. While the rain pelted them, and thunder roared, and lightning filled the sky, Hannah felt like that is what it would be like if she had been swept away into his time. If she had woken up in the 1700s, he would whizz her through the woods on an adventure. But who was she kidding? She would take running water over and liberation over a romanticized idea of the past any day.

As they ran up onto the porch, Hannah was panting and sucking in air as rain dripped off her. Graham looked barely exerted but was dripping with water. He smiled down at Hannah. Once Hannah caught her breath a bit, he reached down, cupped her face, and kissed her. A soft, respectful kiss.

"Why don't you come in and get dried off? I think my brother has some spare clothes in here that will fit you," she said as she shivered.

This rain was cold, late October rain. He nodded, and they headed inside.

CHAPTER 14

"I'm gonna go hop in the shower to warm up and put on some dry clothes. There are towels in the closet and clothes in my brother's room," she called as she headed up the stairs.

Graham found the towels and went into Brett's room to find something dry to put on. He slipped into a soft white T-shirt and some gray Adidas sweatpants. He pulled his wet hair into a knot and put it back with one of Hannah's hair ties. While he put his wet clothes into the dryer and then he thought about Hannah. He thought about how she shivered on the porch, so he got to work making a fire in the fireplace. Once he got that going, he put on the kettle for tea.

Then his thoughts drifted to Hannah on the blanket. The noises and faces she had made as he explored her body and brought her pleasure. He needed to do that again. He could do that for her forever. She was so in charge and capable. Seeing her coming undone at his mere touch was an amazing feeling. She had appeared to be on the edge of something he wasn't even sure women could do.

He heard her come down the stairs, and he turned to see

her. She was in plaid pajama pants and a sweatshirt. The sweatshirt was baggy, but he could see the heaviness of her breasts a little lower, and he knew she wasn't wearing anything beneath that sweatshirt. He shook his head and distracted himself.

"Tea?" he asked.

"Yeah, that would be great. And you made a fire? This is nice." She smiled at him.

"I aim to please ye," he said as he came out from behind the kitchen counter and handed her a warm cup of tea.

Hannah's eyes fell below his waist and lingered there for a moment too long. Graham looked down and saw the pants accentuated his manhood.

"Ye like what ye see?" he asked with a smirk on his face.

Squeezing her eyes shut, she gave her head a little shake, embarrassment playing across her features.

"Me . . . what? . . . Oh! No. I wasn't . . . I was just . . ."

"That's all right. You can admire me."

"Oh, you are so full of yourself," she said. Although, that remark had lost all the edge it once held when she would say those things to him in the previous weeks. That night, they were accompanied by a soft smile. A smile that melted Graham, and at the same time, stirred something protective in him. The protective side was a feeling he was very familiar with but didn't feel necessary. He would spend that protective energy to make her happy because she could keep herself safe. He just wanted to be useful to her. If she didn't need him, he needed to be wanted by her.

"The temperature dropped when the storm blew in. Let's get you warmed up by the fire, lass," he said.

They walked over to the couch, and he put a soft blanket around her. As he sat, Hannah tucked herself in next to him, and he put his arm around her.

"So, I have been thinking," she said.

She gazed into the fire, not meeting Graham's eyes.

"Okay, so you are here for another four months or so. We definitely have a mutual attraction, but this is going to be short-term, no matter how we look at it. You are busy during the day with the horses and helping Sam out. I am finally writing the book I have always wanted to write. But we are drawn to each other," she said, fidgeting with the fringe of the blanket, eyes still on the fire.

"Why don't we just stop fighting it. Just give in to the attraction and spend our time together. Maybe we can learn from each other. Let's just make it not complicated and be with each other for these months we have left together."

Something stirred inside of him. He wanted anything that meant him being close to Hannah, both in bed and out of bed. He enjoyed her immensely in all aspects of who she was. But he also knew that, if he did that, it would be harder to leave her. He knew he already had major feelings for her. He knew that, if they were back in his time, he would already have made her his wife. But it was more complicated—more goes into it. Not to mention, he would be leaving in the spring, which is something he had been trying to ignore more and more lately.

But how could he say no to this woman? This amazing, smart, beautiful, and downright sexy woman curled up next to his side? He could have stayed in that moment, there with her, forever, but they did not have forever. That thought deflated him.

Hannah turned and saw that deflated look on his face. "It's just a thought . . . we don't have to do it." She looked away from him and sipped her tea.

He looked down at her. He took her chin in his hand and lifted it up slightly so she would look at him. "I am here for ye in any way ye wish. Our lives would be different if we belonged to each other's time. If I belonged here, I would date ye and build the lasting relationship this day in age requires. If you were in my time, I would wed ye and protect ye from all harm for the rest of our days. But we are not bound to the love of either of our times. We can make it, so it works for us. I will be anything ye wish for the remainder of my time here."

"Oh . . . are you sure?"

"If it makes ye happy, mo ghrádh, I am sure."

She settled back into him, resting her head on his shoulder. He leaned his head against hers. It felt good. It felt right. They fit together like puzzle pieces.

He had grown accustomed some of the conveniences of the modern day but longed for home. The beauty of his land, the quietness of the past. The modern world was just so loud and fast, and he didn't care for that. But he didn't want to think about leaving Hannah forever. That was a painful thought, so he pushed it away.

He lifted his head, and she looked up at him. He bent his head and kissed her, the gentlest, lightest, barely-there kiss, simply because he could.

Hannah sat up and looked at him, a look Graham loved to see. It was Hannah, looking content and happy.

"I know the cot in the stable office can't be very comfortable, and it is getting colder. Why don't you just sleep here? We can keep each other warm."

The look she gave him warmed him clear down to his toes.

He nodded. "If it pleases ye."

"It does," she said, leaning in for a kiss.

"Now, why don't we go to bed?" she whispered in his ear.

He could feel the heat of her breath, her damp hair falling on his shoulder. She stood and held out her hand. She took it and led him upstairs. That night, they slept together for the first time, but that was it. He would not push her. He would make sure that he knew how a modern woman should be treated, so they kissed—a lot—then went to sleep.

THE NEXT MORNING, Graham woke up holding Hannah's curvy body. He lay there on the softest bed he had ever slept on. They sure didn't have beds like this in his time, but even more wonderful than that was the girl still sleeping in his arms. He had one arm around her waist, holding her close to him. He was glad she was still asleep because the state of his arousal was definitely something Hannah would feel pushing into the globes of her perfect arse. *This is it*, he thought. *This is perfection.*

She stirred, and Graham took one last sniff of her hair. The scent of the shampoo still lingering and intoxicating, then he started to pull away because he didn't want Hannah to feel how hard he was pressed up against her. As he pulled away, she woke up. She turned and looked at him, her hair all a mess and sleep still in her eyes.

"Good morning," she purred.

"Good mornin', mo ghrádh," he said and pressed a kiss to her temple.

He laid on his back, and Hannah put her head on his chest. He put his arm around her, and she absent-mindedly traced his bare chest.

"I could get used to this," she said.

"Aye, me, too. Are you hungry? I could go make some breakfast?"

"No," she whined. "We cannot leave this bed. It is so warm and cozy," she said as she tightened her arm around him.

"How about this? You stay here and be warm and cozy, and I'll go get us some food."

Graham went down to the kitchen, started the coffee machine, then got some eggs out of the refrigerator. He had mastered kitchen basics, so eggs, bacon, toast, and coffee it was. He was still amazed by the convenience of some of the items in the kitchen. Some of them seemed like they were just as much trouble as doing it the old way. But then running water—yeah, he really hoped that invention would be coming along soon.

He stopped and looked out the window, the smell of coffee and bacon filling the air. The leaves had turned and were starting to drop. He'd been there for over six weeks. He was getting used to some of the technology, but he still missed home. He missed knowing what to do, how things worked, and how to behave in most situations. He still felt off balance, but something about this time called to him. Something about this time felt like home.

Then, of course, there was Hannah. The thought of Hannah, marrying Hannah, Hannah being with child, the act of making Hannah be with child, Hannah's soft, supple naked body . . .

What's that smell? Graham snapped back into reality as the bacon burned. "Ock," he said as he threw away the bacon and started some fresh.

He managed to keep his attention on the task at hand. He took Hannah up some breakfast, and she was on her phone.

"Hey, Poppy just texted, 'karaoke tonight at the Elbow Room?'"

"I dinna ken what any of those words mean, but why not?"

"It's gonna be fun. You'll see."

"Of that, mo ghrádh, I have no doubt."

Then he bent his head down and gave her a kiss.

CHAPTER 15

*H*annah and Graham walked into the Elbow Room, a dive bar that had wonderful energy and karaoke. Hannah watched as Graham took in his surroundings. They found Poppy, Sam, and Jackson and made their way over to the table.

Hannah started to pull chairs over to join them. Graham, of course, helped the second he saw what she was doing.

"Let me get that for ye," Graham said.

"Oh, thanks." She smiled at him.

This was their first outing as a couple . . . well, kind of a couple. Whatever they were doing felt different. It felt incredible. It felt like they had been doing it forever, but Hannah was not acknowledging those thoughts. They were on a time clock, and it was ticking even faster these last few days.

"Hey guys! Hannah, you better drink now, I already signed us up," Poppy shouted, drowning out a seemingly drunk woman with big blonde hair, who sang an off-key rendition of "Strawberry Wine."

"Oh, yeah? What for?" Hannah asked.

"You know what for!" Poppy called back.

Graham was sitting close to Hannah, so close their legs were touching, his arm draped around the back of her chair. His big presence was something Hannah was always acutely aware of but because she longed to be closer, not out of the necessity of making sure an ancient highlander didn't get himself into modern-day trouble. Somewhere in the last few weeks, she learned to trust Graham to handle himself.

"Can I get you a drink?" Graham whispered in her ear.

"Umm, yeah . . . Do you know the protocol and everything?"

"We had pubs in my day, mo ghrádh, I believe I can figure it out,"

"All right, get me a jack and coke"

Graham scooted his chair back and headed up to the bar. Poppy leaned over to the table.

"Hey, I haven't talked to you in a while. How are things going? You guys look pretty cozy!"

"Yeah, I don't really know. It's hard to explain."

"Okay, well, try."

Graham saved her from that and slid in next to her with their drinks.

"M'lady," Graham said as he set her drink down.

"Thanks," she said, scooting closer to him, as he settled his arm on the back of her chair.

Poppy gave Hannah a knowing glance, and Hannah rolled her eyes.

Hannah picked up the sticky songbook and flipped through the pages. While some karaoke bars had upgraded to modern equipment and the countless choices of digital music, The Elbow Room still had sticky books from having been spilled on too many times, with song choices that stopped somewhere in the early 2000s. It was perfectly kitschy.

Jackson came back from the bar with his hands full. He set down five shot glasses rimmed with salt and a tiny lime wedge on each one.

"Tequila!" he shouted.

"Ummmm . . . you guys have to know tequila is not my friend," Hannah piped up. "Do you remember the last time?"

"We do," said Sam as he grabbed her hand across the table. "And I would pay money to see that again."

Graham gave Sam a quizzical look.

"Last time we were here, your girl over there may have been a little too close with Jose and ended up dancing on the bar," Sam said.

"It happened one time!" Hannah protested.

"Yes! And it was the best night of my life. Drink!" Jackson said, pushing the shots around the table.

Graham's eyebrows drew together, and a frown found his face.

"Who's Jose?" Graham asked.

The whole table chuckled.

"This is Jose," Hannah said, holding up the shot glass.

"Ahhh, I ken yer meaning."

Jackson licked the salt from the shot glass, tossed down the shot, and sucked on the lime.

Graham looked at him with bewilderment again.

"Lick, shoot, suck, baby."

Graham watched as they all licked off the salt and took their shots followed by their limes.

"I'm supposed to lick this?" he asked Hannah.

"Yep! You are going to lick the salt off, drink the shot, and then suck on the lime."

Hannah could see his apprehension. She squeezed his leg and winked.

"Bottom's up!" yelled Jackson as Graham licked the salt and took the shot.

Hannah watched Graham's face contort.

"Suck this!" she said, shoving the lime in his mouth.

After a moment, Graham looked at her. "You do this on purpose?"

"Ummm . . . not usually, only on special karaoke occasions." Hannah smiled at him.

Graham chuckled and tucked a loose strand of hair behind her ear. Hannah felt a flutter in her tummy, and she couldn't tell if it was from Graham or the tequila.

"Up next, we have Josh," the karaoke announcer called.

Hannah turned as Josh Turner took the stage. The beginning notes to "Friends in Low Places" started, erupting the placed into cheers. Josh was a popular guy—and for good reason. He was one of those people who just had a way with people. He was probably six foot two and solid. He had on jeans, boots, a flannel shirt, and a baseball hat, just as she remembered him.

Memories about Josh made her blush. Josh was a fling in the summer between her senior year of college and law school. After Hannah went back to the city in the fall, they broke it off with no hard feelings, and last she heard, he was engaged. He was one of the better guys Hannah had ever dated. The timing was just wrong.

The entire bar joined him in his song. It is always a crowd-pleaser, and so was he. Hannah could see the moment he winked right at her in the crowd, and by the look on Graham's face, he saw it, too. After the song ended, he made his way over to their table.

"Hey there, city girl! Long time no see!" he said, leaning in for a long hug. "What are you doing out here in this neck of the woods?"

"I quit my job, and I'm staying at the farmhouse for a while."

"You mean we got you out here for a couple of months? We should get together and catch up sometime."

"I'm Graham. Nice to meet you," Graham said, putting his hand out to give him what appeared to be a very firm handshake.

Hannah looked over to Graham, who had been staring Josh down.

"Oh, yeah, sorry. Josh, this is Graham. Graham, Josh. Graham is running our stable right now."

"Aye." He gave Hannah a look she couldn't read. "Is that all I do? I think I take care of a little more than the horses."

"Nice to meet you, man," Josh said, unfazed by the awkward exchange. "Where are you from?"

"Scotland."

"Oh, yeah? How long have you been on this side of the pond?"

"A while," he said, still glaring. He slid his hand from the back of Hannah's chair down around her waist and pulled her in close to him.

"All right . . . well, Hannah, good to see you. Nice to meet you, Graham. Jackson, Sam, Poppy, I hope you will all grace us with your rendition of "Love Shack" tonight. I'll see you around." He nodded and headed back to the bar.

"What was that about?" Hannah whispered to Graham. He seemed jealous. What Hannah once would have described as brutish she had found . . . . endearing? No, that couldn't be right.

"What are you referring to?" he asked with a wily smirk on his face. Hannah wanted to kiss that look right off his face.

"Next up, we have Poppy and Hannah."

Hannah groaned.

"Are you guys doing the routine?" Sam asked, giddiness danced behind his eyes.

"No," Hannah said.

"Yes!" Poppy grinned. She took Hannah's hand and pulled her toward the stage.

"I am not drunk enough for the routine."

"Come on! Tell me that you want to, that you really really want to." Poppy beamed at her.

"Get up on that stage and show your girl power!" Jackson encouraged in a horrible English accent.

They clapped and cheered.

Graham looked at them, clearly missing something, but seemed amused nonetheless.

"Routine?" he asked.

"When they were in fifth grade, they made a dance routine to the Spice Girls. Every now and then, we can get them to do it," Sam said to Graham.

Graham smiled over at Hannah. She groaned and gulped the rest of her drink. Poppy pulled her the rest of the way up on stage and shoved the microphone in her hand.

It really was amazing that, after twenty years, this routine was still so easy to pull out. They brought the house down—because of course they did. What is not to love about the Spice Girls and choreography? Karaoke bar frequenters eat that stuff up.

When they went back to the table, Jackson was there with another round of shots. Hannah looked over at Graham, who was watching her with a big smile on his face. Graham was a jovial fellow. Hannah often heard him laugh and joke, and a smile found his face frequently, but this one looked different. This looked like joy and a smile he felt in his soul. It sent a tingle straight to her heart . . . and maybe somewhere a little lower.

Sam and Jackson cheered as they sat, and Poppy bowed.

"That was something, mo ghrádh," Graham said. He couldn't stop smiling down at her.

"Yeah, we had pretty good moves for fifth graders."

"I like watching your moves now," he said. Then he traced his finger along her cheek and ducked to kiss her. It was a chaste kiss because he was aware of onlookers, but the heat between them had risen. Hannah looked at him, and for just a moment; it was the two of them, the bar falling away.

"All right, Hannah and the highlander over there, these shots aren't going to do themselves!" Jackson yelled over the music.

Hannah snapped back into reality, realizing more people crowded the place than her and Graham and feeling slightly disappointed about it. And, once again, down the hatch, lick, shoot, suck. Hannah's head swam.

"Hey Hannah, I gotta go to the bathroom," Poppy said to her with a knowing look.

"What?"

"The bathroom."

"Oh right," Hannah pushed her chair out to go accompany Poppy to the bathroom.

Graham instinctively stood—because that is what you do when a lady stands . . . in 1745. Hannah looked at him and cocked her head.

"Oh, I'm just going to get us another round of drinks," Graham said.

Poppy pulled Hannah into the bathroom. They made their way into a tiny one-stall bathroom that smelled like cigarette smoke and cheap, fruity perfume. Graffiti decorated the walls, telling people who had the biggest dick and who was a cheating fuckhead, complete with a toilet you could never trust to flush properly.

"Okay, dish," Poppy said.

"I don't know what you are talking about." She attempted to feign innocence, but who was she kidding? Certainly not Poppy.

"Yes, you do! What is going on with you and Graham? He totally marked his territory with Josh, and it looked like you were just about to jump each other's bones out there. When did you guys start doing it?"

"What?! We are not doing it?"

"Are you serious?" Poppy said, clearly taken aback.

"Ummm, yeah . . . I think I would know if I got laid, and I definitely haven't gotten laid. We slept in the same bed last night, we kiss all the damn time, we came close to something at the wedding and, then the last night, when the storm happened, but no . . . just kissing . . . And a little bit of groping."

Poppy looked at Hannah, her mouth agape, shaking her head.

"That is not the energy you guys have?"

"I know, right!?" Hannah said, feeling the exasperation she had been trying to push back at their lack of doin' it.

"So, you want to do it?"

"Yeah, I do!" Hannah blurted, admitting it for the first time. "Okay, I must be drunk, but yeah, I do. I mean, you know how weird this whole thing is with Graham, so it's complicated."

"Nope, not complicated. You need to get some of that fine Scottish ass."

"You think?"

"What do you have to lose? Take some advice from the bathroom sages before us," Poppy said, pointing to the wall.

"What, I should call Dylan for good head?"

"No, this one, ya weirdo." She pointed to a piece of graffiti in pink sparkly lettering that read "Carpe this Muthafuckin' Diem!"

"You're right! I am going to tell him."

"All right, let's go, Hannah."

When they left the bathroom, Hannah scanned the bar for

Graham, her liquid courage aiding her in her quest. He was still not at the table. She searched and found him at the bar. He was standing there with some woman, the big-haired "Strawberry Wine"-singing woman, to be precise, who was batting her eyes. She also had her hand resting on Graham's forearm.

Hannah saw red. She could not remember ever being jealous like that before, but she stormed over to Graham.

"Hi, I'm Hannah," she said abruptly, butting into their conversation, offering her hand for a greeting.

The woman smiled at Hannah, and Graham looked down at her, surprised.

"Hi, Hannah, I'm Heather. I was just talking to Graham here. Did you know he's from Scotland? He has the cutest accent," she said, tracing her fingers on his arm.

"Yeah, I know he's from Scotland. He is here with me." She laced her arm through his, staking her claim.

"He's with you?" the woman looked at her, surprised.

"Yup!" Hannah said, popping the *p*, looking her square in the eyes.

Graham looked at Hannah and smiled. He may have even chuckled, but Hannah couldn't be bothered with that.

"Oh . . . okay."

"Bye, Heather!" Hannah said to her abruptly.

The woman looked at her, huffed, and flipped her hair before walking away.

"Why, Hannah Glenn, are ye jealous?" Graham looked down with an almost gleeful look on his face.

"What? I am not!" she insisted.

"Ye are," Graham beamed down at her.

"I do not know what you are talking about."

"Oh, yes, ye do, but let me just say, if I had behaved the way ye just did ye would have treated me as if I were a brute."

Hannah dropped her head. She wanted to fight, but he was right.

"Well, you were jealous early tonight!"

"Aye, I was, but I'm not the one who claims to be above such behavior. Back in my day, I'd fight a man for looking at ye like he did, let alone embracing ye so."

Hannah looked at him, crossed her arms, and huffed.

"Oh, dinna go lookin' cross. Just admit ye want to claim me as much as I want to claim you." He looked at her face and cocked an eyebrow.

"Well, . . . okay, so I was jealous. Are you happy?"

"Aye. That must have been painful for ye to admit. Do ye need to sit down?" he said, openly mocking her. "But, mo ghrádh, ye must ken by now. I am always happy with ye. And just so ye ken, no other woman in this century, or any other for that matter, is anywhere near as bonny as you."

He bent down and claimed her mouth before putting his hands on her hips and pulling her closer to him. Hannah opened her mouth and deepened the kiss. She ran her hands up his arms and into his hair, holding him close. Graham's hands slid down to the swells of Hannah's ass and pulled her even closer. She could feel his hardening cock pressing into her belly.

The world fell away, the noise in the bar, the people brushing past; it was just Hannah and Graham existing in a perfect kiss. Hannah broke the kiss, but Graham continued to kiss down her jaw and neck.

"Take me home, highlander," she murmured in his ear.

Graham pulled back and looked at her. She looked at him in a way that there could be no question about what she intended to do when they got home.

"As ye wish," he said. "Should we say goodbye to yer friends?"

"Yeah."

They headed over to the table.

"Hey, guys, I think we are headed home."

"Yeah, you are!" Poppy yelled in a knowing way, wagging her eyebrows. Hannah shot her a look, and Poppy just smiled back.

"How are you getting home? You shouldn't drive," Sam said, always being the big brother of the group.

Hannah raised the phone in her hand. "Already on it."

Sam nodded his approval. "I'll see you tomorrow?" he asked Graham.

"Aye, I'll be over once I am done with the horses."

"Unless he is otherwise occupied, right, Han!" Poppy said. Hannah shot a shut-the-hell-up look to her best friend.

"Did someone call an Uber?" Josh Turner said with a jovial smile on his face.

Graham turned and eyed him, and Hannah thought she even heard a low growl.

"Ummm . . . yeah?" Hannah said slowly.

Josh held up his phone, showing the Uber app. "Welp, here I am."

"You're our driver?" she asked.

"Yep, there are only a couple of us drivers in town, and I'm here so let me know when you're ready."

Graham muttered something in Gaelic, and Hannah elbowed him.

"This is too perfect!" Poppy said, clearly amused. "We all need to hang out more."

"Good night, Poppy," Hannah said, shaking her head.

"I will call you tomorrow."

"I don't doubt it! Later." Hannah said as Graham helped her into her jacket, and they followed Josh out the door.

CHAPTER 16

*G*raham had been quiet the whole ride home with his hand on Hannah's knee, eyes boring into the back of Josh's headrest. Hannah found the whole thing amusing, and she hated to admit Graham was right. If he had behaved that way a few weeks prior, Hannah would have had a few choice words for him, but she just found it entertaining.

When they pulled up to the farmhouse, Hannah said her goodbyes to Josh. Graham was already out and opened her door. She stood, and Graham shut it behind her.

The realization that he had opened all the doors, paid for all the drinks, and been a perfect gentleman the whole night took her by surprise. He also got along well with all her friends. Hannah couldn't remember many dates that went that way.

And to think, only a few weeks prior, Hannah thought him to be a hopeless brute. Sure, he was close to ravishing her at the bar, and sure, she had secretly wished he would have just heaved her up on the bar and done dirty things to her. But it was only a wish, and if she had gotten her way once inside the house, it would be reality.

"I had an enjoyable time tonight with ye, Hannah," Graham said as he smiled down at her. His hand rested on the small of her back as she put the key in the lock and opened the door. They walked in, and Hannah kicked off her shoes.

"It doesn't have to be over yet," Hannah said. She looked at him with the same fire in her eyes as she did at the bar.

"I think we need to talk first, Hannah."

"No more talking." Hannah fisted his shirt in her hands and walked him back until his ass hit the counter. She reached up and kissed him.

He pulled his head up and put his hands on her shoulders. "Hannah, wait."

"Why, Graham? Don't you want to do more than kiss me? You seem to like me. I mean, you seem like you are attracted to me."

"Be assured it is not a lack of desire," he said. Hannah felt something poking her belly that told her his words were true.

"Then, what?" she asked.

"Hannah . . . I just want to make sure it is what you want. I am leaving soon, and you were the one who said you didn't want things to be complicated."

"This won't complicate things."

"How could it not? You could become with child. Then, what would we do?"

Hannah smiled up at him. "Well, if that is your only concern, I can tell you I am on the pill."

"The pill?" His brows pinched as he looked down at her, her eyes still burning with passion.

"Yes, the pill. Birth control. I take it, so I won't get pregnant until I am ready."

"The future has thought of everything." He shook his head.

"Yes," Hannah said, as she tried to kiss him again.

He pulled back.

"Well, there is something else I must tell you before we proceed further."

Hannah stopped and looked at him. His tone sounded different, and although she was ready to take things to the next level, he might not have been. That was something that deserved her full attention.

"Well, I gather you have experience in such things, being a modern woman and all. I am not a modern man. I have not engaged in such activities before, and I do very much want to do them with you, but I just want to make sure it is what ye truly want. And, mo ghrádh, I dinna want our first time together to be done when ye've had too much to drink."

Hannah smiled. He was perfect. How on earth could she ever have thought otherwise?

"Okay, I hear you." She took a step back to give this conversation the space it needed. Graham stopped her and held her against him. "We can take our time with this decision. Also, I am not drunk anymore, Graham . . . Okay, maybe still a little tipsy, but I have wanted you probably since the moment I saw you, but definitely since you kissed me in that hotel room. We don't have to do anything you aren't ready for. But if you want, there are other things we can do, ya know, other than just kissing. But only if you want to."

"I do have one more question for ye," he muttered.

Hannah looked up at him to see he was flushed, turning redder by the minute.

"Are you blushing?" she asked. She reached up to touch his cheek and could feel the heat under her hand.

"We have watched movies together, where people were . . . coupling." He paused.

"We have," she said, trying to help him get out whatever he was trying to say.

"In my time . . . well . . . clearly, things are different now. It used to be seen as something men enjoyed, and of course, to conceive bairns. But modern women seem to like it, and it seems in the movies, that some women have a large amount of pleasure . . . I was just wondering if that is what it is supposed to be like. Am I supposed to make ye feel that?"

Okay, she finally got it. He was nervous and apparently didn't know about orgasms.

"Yes, Graham, women can feel the same pleasure as men from sex. Well, to be fair, I don't know if it's the same pleasure, but women can have orgasms just like men. And yes, I'm sure you will make me feel like that. I know that because I came close to having one last night outside from just your hands on my body and your mouth on me. I know you will because you care enough to try. That is all you need to be a good lover, the desire to please your partner, and a little bit of patience."

Graham nodded.

"Is there anything else?"

"No, I think that covers it," he said before dropping a small kiss down on her mouth.

"We can keep taking it slow, Graham, if that is what you want, no pressure."

"Well, I think, maybe it is time we took the next step," he said with a half smile.

"Oh, thank God, I have been dying to get my hands on you and see you naked."

Graham grunted his approval and pulled her in close, kissing her, his hands splayed wide on her ass.

"Anything to please ye, Hannah. You and this arse of yers."

She hit him on the chest with mock disapproval, and he nipped her ear. Then she kissed him. This kiss was the same heat as their kiss in the bar. Things were going to move that night, and she was so ready for it.

"Come upstairs with me," she said in a low, sultry tone.

She could feel the heat of his gaze as they climbed the stairs. She made her way to her bedroom and turned on the lamp by her bed. Graham leaned against the doorway, watching her, his eyes hooded, his erection visibly straining against his jeans.

He made his way over to her bed and sat on the edge. Hannah walked over to him and stood between his legs. Graham put his hands on her ass again.

"I could hold on to this perfect round arse my whole life. Just never let it go," he said, giving it a squeeze.

"You have to let go of my ass to touch other parts of me."

Hannah looked down at him and bit her bottom lip. With him seated on the bed, and her standing between his legs, his head was level with her breasts. He let go of her ass and brought his hand around to give one of her breasts a gentle squeeze. Then he slid his hands down and rested them on her hips.

"Hannah, it is important to me that I be a good lover and know how to please ye. Can ye show me?"

"What?" Hannah breathlessly answered him.

"Tonight, I want you to show me how ye like to be touched and how to please ye. Do ye think you can do that for me? I want to take care of ye and bring ye pleasure."

"Graham . . ."

Hannah's mind was racing. She looked away. She wasn't new to sex, and she wasn't even new to asking for what she wanted in bed. Hannah had her fair share of bad sex before she had learned to speak up and be an active partner, letting her wants and needs be heard, but never like this. This was more intimate. She looked back down at him.

He gazed at her with sincerity. "Please, Hannah, show me what to do."

Hannah swallowed the lump in her throat and nodded. She dropped her head to kiss him. He pulled her close and embraced her. She pulled back enough to slip her shirt over her head. Graham watched as Hannah reached behind and undid the clasp of her bra.

He inhaled a sharp breath when Hannah slid it off and let it drop to the floor. She could feel the heat of his breath on her nipple, and she started to ache inside. Hannah reached down, took his hand, and put it on her breast.

"How about this for a start?" she said.

Graham squeezed and watched the nipple constrict between his fingers. He leaned forward and let his tongue trace over her nipple, inducing a moan out of her. Graham looked at her with one eyebrow cocked like he was going to devour her. He cupped her other breast. The look of awe on his face made Hannah blush. She had never felt this adored in her life.

He held her like she was the most precious thing, but his eyes looked at her like he was a wolf and she was his prey. His heated gaze found her eyes. He licked her nipple. Then he put his mouth over it, this time letting more of the nipple in his mouth and sucked. Hannah let out another moan, this one a bit louder. He squeezed the other breast, then moved it to his mouth.

Hannah moved her hand to the hem of Graham's shirt and pulled it up. She needed to see him, to feel him.

"I want to look at you and feel your skin against mine."

Graham slipped his shirt off over his head and stood. Hannah looked at his body, her eyes burning with desire.

"Wow" was all she could say when she looked at him.

"Wow indeed," he said, looking at her. He reached for the button of her pants. "May I?"

"Yes," Hannah panted, her hands tracing his taut stomach.

Graham undid the button and pushed her pants down over the swell of her hips, and they fell to the floor. Hannah stepped out of them.

"May I?" Hannah asked, finding the button of his jeans.

"Yes, but don't forget. Tonight is all about yer pleasure." She nodded. Graham stood and let Hannah unbutton his jeans. Then they fell to the floor.

Hannah laid down on the bed, and Graham shifted to lie next to her. He held her body close to his. Graham tried to position himself so he would not spear her with his rock-hard cock, but she loved the feel of it. She loved to feel the proof of his attraction.

He let his hands explore her body. He pressed soft kisses on her belly. She was all softness and smoothness, and he seemed to relish in its feel and the give of her flesh to the hardness of his own. His hands roamed, learning every curve, her waist, her ass, her tits, and her glorious, soft belly. All of this would have made her uncomfortable in the past, but with Graham, it felt different. It felt like he was worshipping her, learning her.

"Where should I touch you?" he whispered in her ear.

"Anywhere."

"Even here?" he asked, sliding his hand down to the fullest part of her belly, his hand drifting beneath her underwear's elastic band.

"Especially there," she moaned before nibbling his ear.

"Show me."

Hannah had never had a man even ask what she liked before, let alone ask her to show him. She wasn't quite sure what to do. She pushed away the self-conscious voice about her body and about asking for what she wanted. She knew

Graham well enough to know he really did want to please her.

Hannah gently took his hand and slid it under the stretchy fabric of her underwear.

"Touch me here," she said.

He looked at Hannah with intensity. She slid his hands down until it was cupping her warm, slippery sex. Hannah wiggled the panties down around her hips, and Graham used his other hand to work them down off her body.

Hannah could feel her heart pound and her insides turning to liquid just with the thought of what his hands were about to do.

Hannah started exploring herself. Graham followed, feeling what her hands were doing. She slipped her fingers into the folds, and Graham's fingers followed. She let out a moan, and he bent and kissed her mouth.

She could tell she was not going to take long this time. She pushed one finger inside of her. Graham's followed. He looked at her like he was trying to figure out a puzzle, a puzzle that would break her into a million pieces.

She pulled out her finger and slid them up to her clit. His finger followed again. She started making slow circles, and so did he. Hannah began to lose herself. At some point, Graham took over, and Hannah's hand fell away. Graham, once again, slipped one finger inside, then two, sliding them in and out of her. Hannah had to admit: he was a natural, and she was getting so close.

"Do you like that?" he asked.

"Yes," Hannah said, panting.

Graham looked at her and bit his lip, then he smirked. He fucking smirked at her while she was just about to come on his hand. He grazed her clit with his thumb as he worked his fingers inside of her. At that touch, her back arched, and she moaned and closed her eyes.

Graham must have noticed the way her body reacted to the touch because he didn't let up. He started his thumb making slow, tight circles while his fingers worked inside of her. Hannah felt the warm liquid sensation spreading from her belly up into her chest. Then she lost it. She felt her entire body tingle and pulse. She cried out. Hannah fell to pieces on Graham's hand. She opened her eyes as Graham was looking at her like she was the center of his universe.

"Wow . . ." was all Hannah could say again.

"Making ye make those noises is something I could do for the rest of my life," Graham said.

He leaned down and kissed her as she tried to come back into this world. She gazed at him as he lay propped up next to her. He was so confident and so gentle. She knew there was so much more to this man.

She brushed her thumb against his cheek. She could feel the slight scratch of his stubble growing, a reminder of a real man in her bed, but that thought led her to the thought of the unreal situation and expiration date of their time together. She brought her other hand to Graham and reached for his hard cock. He stopped her and shook his head.

"No, not yet, mo ghrádh. Like I said, tonight is all about you." He dipped his head and kissed her.

Hannah had never been with a man who was so intent on her pleasure. Most of the time, her pleasure was an afterthought to theirs, but not with Graham. She ran her hand up his strong back and down his strong arms.

She had asked the witch for her perfect man, but she really didn't know it could be like this. Tears pooled in the corner of her eyes, and she tried to blink them away. A renegade tear made its way down her cheek.

"Are you crying, lass? Was it bad?"

"No, it was perfect. You are perfect. Why do we have to exist in different centuries?"

"I'm afraid I dinna have an answer to that, but last night, ye said we should make the most of the time we have together. And if ye still mean that, and this is something ye want, Hannah, let me make ye happy while I can."

Tears streamed from her face. How could someone, who had made her as angry as he had, have been so unbelievably perfect?

"Hush, mo ghrádh, dinna fash."

He wiped the tear and whispered Gaelic words in her ear.

"I'm sorry," she sniffed. "Tequila always makes me weepy . . . well, tequila and, apparently, thoughtful men."

He smiled warmly at her and traced her features.

"What does that mean? Mo-ghry, you always say that, and I don't know what it means."

"It is a term of endearment, which translates to 'my love.'"

"I like that," she said thoughtfully. She reached up and held the hand that had been tracing her face. She leaned into his hand, leading his hand to cradle her face. "And I like you, Graham. I have never felt this before. This, what exists between us."

He pressed a soft kiss to her lips.

Hannah closed her eyes. Where in the world did that honesty come from? That kind of honesty was something Poppy generally had to force out of her, but she had just offered it to Graham. She would like to blame the liquor, but she knew she no longer felt drunk. She felt . . . love.

Things just got complicated.

CHAPTER 17

*H*annah was in full-on Thanksgiving mode. Thanksgiving was the next day, and she had spent all week preparing. She was cooking and cleaning and making sure everything would be perfect. She had lists. Her lists had lists. She was ready. She hadn't seen any of her family since the game day debacle. She also hadn't spoken to her father, which was not like them. She was nervous. But right then, she was watching tv, the weather channel to be precise.

A cold rush of air blew in as the door opened. Graham entered the kitchen, snow swirling behind him. He quickly shut the door, stomped his boots on the rug by the door, and shook the snow from his hair.

"Ock, it's comin' down out there. I think we are in for one helluva storm," he said as he bent down to slip off his boots. He walked over to Hannah to join her. He put his hands on her shoulders and gently massaged them.

"Is that the storm?" he asked, looking amazed at the TV.

"Yeah, it looks like we are in for a Nor'Easter. We haven't

had one this big in a while. My sister's flight has already been canceled."

"What about the rest of yer family? Do ye think they will make it?"

"If my parents have left already . . . maybe, but not my brother. He wasn't supposed to be in until tomorrow morning."

Hannah couldn't decide if she was relieved or disappointed. She liked Thanksgiving enough, but it was a lot of work, and she and her mother would primarily do the work. And given her mother's food issues, it always put her on edge.

"I called and texted my mom, but I haven't heard back yet."

Graham continued to rub her back while she watched the TV. "The horses are bedding down. It's gonna be a big one."

"Yeah, it looks like we might get up to four feet of snow. I've never been here when we had a storm that big. I know we have a kit somewhere. I'll have to find it."

"Well, I have plenty of firewood stacked outside. I might try and set more on the porch, or maybe in the garage."

"Yeah, we might lose power for a while. I know that happens."

Graham looked at her. Hannah had her arms crossed, one hand tapping her arm incessantly. Graham covered that fidgeting hand with his own.

"What has ye worried so, lass?"

"I don't know . . . I mean we are in for a big storm. Tomorrow is Thanksgiving. I haven't heard from my parents. I want them here, but god help us all if we get snowed in with them. We have all this food. What do I do with all the food? Do I need to go get gas for generators? Do we even have them? If so, how do they work?"

"All that is goin' on up there in that wee head of yers?" He smiled down at her and kissed the top of her head.

"Yeah, Graham, I'm trying to hold it together," she said incredulously.

"What happens if ye stop trying to hold it together?"

She stared at him. His statement was so matter-of-fact it didn't compute.

"What do you mean?" she asked.

"What I mean is, what if ye decided to take care of the part ye could take care of and let the rest go?"

She looked at him. He made it sound so easy, but what he was asking was next to impossible.

"Hear me out," he said. "So, we need to find out where yer parents are. I see yer worried about them. Have ye checked in with yer sister or brother?"

"No."

"Here." He picked up her phone and handed it to her. "Work yer magic and call yer brother. Maybe he knows."

She looked at him and took a breath before she typed.

Hannah: Have you heard from mom and dad? I wanna make sure they aren't stuck in this.

Brett: Nope, but if they aren't there, they probably won't make it, the city is in gridlock and already shut down.

Hannah: okay thanks

Brett: I'll let you know if I hear anything.

Hannah: Thanks

Just then, Hannah's phone rang, and a picture of her mother popped up.

"Hello." She answered it quickly.

"Hi, Hannah, it's Mom." That's how she always said hello, like caller ID wasn't a thing.

"Yeah, Mom, it's you. Are you okay? Are you guys coming?"

"We tried, sweetheart, but we couldn't get out of the city. I told your father we should leave last night, but he thought we could beat the storm, so it looks like we're going to have to hunker down here."

"Okay, Mom, thanks. I'm glad you are okay."

"Dad said to tell you that, if you the power goes while you are there, turn off the water upstairs and to the rest of the addition and hang some blankets to store the heat and keep the fire going, and you should be okay."

"Okay, anything else? Can I talk to him?" Hannah asked.

"No, honey, he is out picking up a few things before we can't leave the house again."

"Okay, well, stay safe," Hannah said, feeling defeated.

"You, too, sweetheart. We will see you at Christmas!"

"Bye, Mom."

"Bye."

Hannah put her phone down on the table and sighed.

"Well?" Graham asked.

"They aren't coming. They are stuck in the city."

Hannah had mixed emotions. She wanted to fix things with her father, but part of her was relieved to not have to deal with the stress of another family gathering. She was nervous about the coming storm, but Graham's hand on her back was a steadying presence.

"All right, so I guess it is just you and I weathering the storm together. There are worse things." Graham tried to reassure her.

"We will probably lose power," she said.

"I assure ye I know how to live without electricity. I managed pretty well for myself my whole life without it," he said with a warm smile.

"What about all the food? What am I supposed to do with a giant turkey?"

"Well, I say let's cook it and eat it. That is what it was intended for."

"But if the power goes out, the stuff in the refrigerator will go bad," she insisted.

"Hannah, mo ghrádh, look outside. The world is our refrigerator."

Hannah finally took a breath. She looked at Graham, who looked so calm and sure. Hannah was on edge from preparing for her family. Toss a blizzard into the mix, and she was about ready to blow. But when she looked at him, she realized she had a partner in this. Graham would not let anything bad happen to her, and she didn't have to do it all herself. It was just like he said. Maybe she could try to stop holding it together.

She looked out the window. In that moment, the snow was starting to accumulate, but it was still gently falling.

"Well, it will be a race against time, but if we get the turkey in the oven, maybe we can have Thanksgiving tonight, just us, before the storm is in full swing."

"I think that is a great idea. How can I help?"

And at that, they set to motion to create a Thanksgiving feast for two.

CHAPTER 18

*L*ater that night, they sat to a beautiful meal as the snow blew outside. They had the whole shebang: turkey, mashed potatoes and gravy, green beans, rolls, and pumpkin pie. Sure, it was excessive for just the two of them, but it was one of the most enjoyable evenings they had spent together.

After they had finished eating, he busied himself with scrubbing the pans while Hannah loaded the dishwasher. As they finished, Hannah wiped down the counter and swayed to the music. Graham had been filled with affection for Hannah all through dinner but watching that ass sway filled him with something else.

"Look at it blowing out there. It's really piling up," Hannah said, looking out the kitchen window at the swirling snow.

Graham shook his head, trying to shake off the hypnotism of her ass. He looked out the window, and she was right. The first step of the porch was already buried in snow. The wind blew it all around, and the conditions were near a white-out. The wind whistling outside, and Graham was familiar with snowy weather, having lived in the highlands most of his life, but that storm would still count as one of the most intense snowstorms he had ever seen.

"I'm going to go find all the candles and weather radio, and all that stuff. I know we have some around here somewhere."

"I'll get more firewood."

Graham slid on his coat and boots, and as he opened the door, a gust blew in. He leaned into the wind and walked to the end of the porch to get the firewood. Five inches of snow covered the ground. In a couple of trips, he brought in wood and stacked them next to the fireplace. Hannah came down with a box of candles, flashlights, batteries. They had enough food and bottled water set in. There was nothing left to do but watch the snow.

"What do you want to do?" Hannah asked.

"I have a couple ideas," Graham said, smirking at her.

"I like where your mind is, but I'm way too full for those types of activities. Should we watch a movie before we lose power?"

"Aye, you pick one, and I will tend to the fire."

Hannah picked *White Christmas*, since it seemed like a good movie to watch the night before Thanksgiving with a storm blowing outside. Hannah was all set on the couch, comfy cozy in a blanket. Graham joined her and put his arm around her. She snuggled right in and laid her head on his shoulder. They fit like two puzzle pieces. Graham rested his head on hers, the scent of her hair as appealing as ever. She rested her hand on his leg under the blanket. If she moved it much higher, she would find out just how much Hannah turned him on. Just being next to her had an effect on him.

Just about the time the two men got done singing about

being sisters, the movie cut out. Everything was quiet. Everything went dark except for the glow of the fire.

"Well, there it goes," said Hannah.

"Aye, there it goes. Now, it's like yer living in my time, only with much more comfortable furniture. And much more bonny, good-smellin' lasses," he said as he played with a lock of her blonde curls. Hannah sighed and snuggled in closer to him, and he rubbed her arm.

"Graham, today could have really sucked, with my family not coming for the holiday and things still being weird with my dad. It would have been easy to wallow and feel sorry for myself, but right now, all I'm feeling is thankful you are here."

Graham felt a lump forming in his throat. He knew he was dangerously close to loving this woman. He probably already did, but she had asked for things not to be complicated. So, he pushed back those feelings and tried to stay in the moment. It wasn't too hard because this particular moment may have been one of the best moments of his life.

"And here, we sit. No power, in the middle of a blizzard. I should be going down a list preparing for things that could go wrong, making sure everyone around me is okay, taking care of everyone and everything, but I'm not. I am sitting here, relaxing and snuggling on the couch while a storm rages outside."

She sat up and looked at him. He lifted his hand and brushed her hair behind her ear.

"And do you know why I don't feel like I need to do it all myself? It's because of you. I know nothing bad is going to happen because you are here. I feel calm and cared for the first time in . . . well, maybe forever." Her voice cracked on the last part, and Graham put his hand on her knee to center her. "Thank you, Graham. I know these are really weird circumstances, but I'm really glad you are here."

He lifted his hand to her face, and his thumb grazed her cheek. She felt warm under his hand.

"Aye, I am very glad to be here with ye tonight, Hannah Glenn. Let the storm rage, and we will weather it together here inside."

CHAPTER 19

*H*annah leaned forward and kissed him, with deep urgency. She moved to straddle him. His hands found her ass and pulled her into him. Fisting his hair, she pulled him close. The heat was rising in her. Graham had brought her to orgasm many times. It was time she returned the favor if he was willing. She desperately wanted him inside of her.

She stopped kissing him and sat, straddling him, looking into his eyes. They were hooded with pleasure. His cheeks flushed.

"Graham, you have made me feel so good in so many ways so many times. Please, if you are ready, can I do the same for you?"

Graham nodded and pulled her into a kiss. Hannah pulled her head back.

"Consent is words, Graham," she purred. "Do you want to have sex with me tonight?"

Graham took a deep breath and looked at her with a hungry gaze.

"I very much want to have sex with ye tonight, Hannah Glenn."

Hannah dipped her head back down and kissed him slowly. She licked into his mouth with delicious deliberation. Then she shifted and swung her leg off and stood up. She could hear Graham groan at the loss of contact.

"Upstairs."

The heat in his eyes set her ablaze. He stood instantly and pulled Hannah in for one last kiss before they broke apart. She turned to head upstairs, and Graham grabbed one of the candles that was burning on the mantle and follow upstairs behind her. When they got to the bedroom, she heard the door click behind her. She turned around to see Graham devouring her with his eyes.

"Take your shirt off." He rasped at her.

Without a thought, Hannah put her hands on the hem of her shirt and pulled it over her head.

"Now your pants."

She undid the button of her jeans and shimmied them over her full soft hips, and they hit the floor. She stepped out of them and walked over to Graham. He pulled his shirt off over his head, and Hannah unbuttoned his jeans before pushing them down. His cock sprung out, hard and erect. Hannah felt her throb deep inside of her, causing her to squeeze her thighs. She slid her hand under the elastic of his boxers and felt his hot, hard length, his growl sending shivers of heat through Hannah's entire body.

"Sit on the bed," he rasped at her.

Hannah immediately sat on the bed. Graham kneeled before her and kissed her deeply. He reached behind her and fumbled with the clasp of her bra. For a man from the 1700s, he was quickly getting the hang of unclasping a bra. He slid the straps down her shoulders. As her full breasts came out of the bra, he took them both into his hands. One of his hands gave the nipple a little pinch, and his mouth found the other one, and he sucked it into his mouth. She gave a little moan, and Graham looked at her and licked his lips.

He pulled at her underwear. She shifted her weight so he could slip them off. Then he dropped his head lower and pushed her knees apart.

"Graham, I want you inside of me."

"Patience, mo ghrádh, first I am going to make ye moan for me."

He slipped one finger in between her slippery folds. He swirled her wetness around her engorged clit, and her breath caught in her throat. Then he moved his fingers lower and pushed one inside. He used his other hand to hold her open, and he bent down and gently flicked his tongue over her clit.

Hannah could feel the build of pleasure in her belly. He pushed two fingers inside of her and worked her slowly. He swirled his tongue around her clit. Hannah fell back against the bed, pleasure starting to take over her body. He sucked her clit into his mouth again, swirling his tongue over it while he fucked her with his fingers. Hannah cried out and broke for him. Her body throbbed with pleasure, and he stayed there patiently between her knees, helping her to ride every wave of pleasure.

"Move up the bed," he said, nodding his head, signaling her to scoot up the bed.

Hannah did as he said. She watched as he slid his boxers down, freeing his cock. He gave himself one hard stroke as he watched Hannah slide up and open her legs. He licked his lips. Then he slowly kissed his way up her body. Her calves, her thighs, her belly, her breast until he claimed her mouth. She could taste herself on his lips. He centered himself between her legs, and she could feel his cock at her entrance.

Propping himself on his forearms, he looked at Hannah. "Are ye ready for me?"

"Please. I want to feel you inside of me."

He kissed her and pushed into her. He moaned as he slid in. When he was fully sheathed inside her, he lowered his body and anchored himself to Hannah, one arm under her shoulder, the other at her hips. He ground himself against her with every push. *He has to be a time-traveling sex wizard*, Hannah thought. There was no way this was his first time. She was going to come again, and she so rarely came from penetration.

He picked up speed, and Hannah cried out. He looked down at her, his eyes hungry, bucking his hips into her harder.

"Do ye like that?"

"Yes!"

He pulled almost all the way out and thrust back in, hard. Hannah could feel the pressure building and closed her eyes.

"Look at me, I want to see yer face while you fall apart on my cock."

Hannah opened her eyes, and he thrust back into her. Hannah cried out. He picked up speed and continued thrusting into her harder. She cried out one last time, and pleasure rippled through her body and curled her toes.

He gave two last hard thrusts, then growled, "Hannah."

She could feel his orgasm inside of her while he shuddered on top of her. He bent down and kissed her, a slow, emotional kiss. Hannah was gone. She loved this man. No one had ever made her feel taken care of like he did. And no man had ever made her come like that. Ever.

"Wow . . ." Hannah said.

"I'll say," Graham said as he slid out of her. He lay beside her and adjusted them so that Hannah's head was resting on his chest. She could hear his heart pounding.

"That was amazing, Graham. Are you sure you have never done that before?" she asked, trying to catch her breath.

"I think I would remember something like that. But I am looking forward to doing that again," he said before pressing a kiss to her head.

CHAPTER 20

*G*raham woke up the next morning, still naked and cuddling Hannah, who was sound asleep. He felt triumphant after what they did the night before—two times. A well-sexed, sleepy girl in his arms was a stroke to his ego. He often felt out of place there, so that gave him a welcomed bit of cockiness.

He was warm in bed, but he could see his breath, so he knew the house still didn't have electricity. He wanted Hannah to wake to a warm house. He eased out of bed, taking care not to wake her.

When he got out of bed, he realized just how cold it was. It wasn't freezing, but the cold air on his naked body hit him like an arctic blast.

"Bollocks," he muttered as he slipped on his clothes. He laid another blanket on Hannah and took one last look at her. The sight of her mess of blonde hair spread across the pillow, the curve of her body hidden by blankets, and the thought of their last night together warmed his heart. He smiled and headed downstairs to warm the house, too.

The first thing he did was light some fires. Once he had a

fire going in the kitchen and in the living room, he found the bin Hannah had brought out the day before. He lifted the binder from the bin that was filled with candles, matches, flashlights and batteries, and other things he wasn't quite sure what to do with.

He opened the "Winter Storm - Snowed In" tab in the binder. Graham could tell where Hannah got her love of lists. He found simple easy-to-read, step-by-step instructions. There were even pictures so he could be sure he was doing it correctly. He read the steps and got to work. The tasks seemed to be about shutting off the newer addition of the house from the older part.

He put some tea on for Hannah to warm her when she got up.

"Holy Fuck! It is cold!" he heard Hannah call out from upstairs.

He chuckled to himself. He looked to see her pulling the blanket aside he had hung at the top of the stairs. She emerged, looking grumpy, pulling her hoody around her. Her face softened when she saw him. She looked around at the fire, then back at the blanket.

"What's this?" she asked.

"Ahh, well, I found this," he said, holding up the binder. "I followed the steps for Winter storm, snowed in."

"Did you?" She had a very pleased look on her face.

"Aye, I have water heating up on the fire for tea. Ye might want to check the water shut-off for the addition. I think I did it right, but I'm not sure."

"You did all this? By yourself?"

Her pleased look turned to one of shock.

"Well, there's no one here but me, so I would say so."

Her shock insulted him.

"I'm sorry, I am just shocked. I just didn't expect you to . . . I don't know . . . I mean . . . I guess I'm not used to people doing stuff like this, and with this not being your time—"

"Hannah, I can read. Those directions were simple enough. And let's face it, living without electricity puts us more in my time than yers. I will take care of ye."

That shocked look on her face caused him to bristle. He would show her that he could take care of her. She deserved to be taken care of.

"So, Hannah"—he walked over to her and took her into his arms—"let's start over. Good morning to ye, and I had an amazing night with ye last night."

Hannah looked at him, and with a small smile, melted into his embrace.

Graham pressed a kiss to the top of her head.

Hannah hummed. "You're warm."

"Well, let's see if we can get you warmed back up."

She sat on the couch, and he tucked in blankets around her. Then he took the kettle from over the fire with hot pads and poured them both a cup of tea before joining her on the couch. She held out the blanket to him, inviting him under. She snuggled right into him. He enjoyed the press of her against him, even though they both had on several layers of clothes.

"How much snow did we get?" Hannah asked.

"I'm not entirely certain, but it appears to be quite a sizable amount."

Graham looked out the windows. The snow was up to the sills in some places, but that could be drifts. They would have to get out to see.

"I will probably need to check on the horses today. I gave them plenty of water, and they have enough hay to eat and bedding to stay warm, but I will head out there later today."

"So, dig out to see the horses, but besides that we are snowed in with no power," she said.

"So it would seem, how long does the power outage last?" he asked.

"That depends, sometimes hours, sometimes days, a couple of times a week. Out here in the country, it can take a while."

They sat in comfortable silence, enjoying the fire and the tea's warmth.

"So, this is just an idea, but it intrigues the writer in me. I am snowed in . . . with a highlander from the 1700s. Sure, we could try and get generators and do all that stuff. But what if we leaned into it?"

Graham looked at her with his hand, absentmindedly tracing her arm.

"I'm not certain I follow."

"Let's pretend we are living in your time. I mean this part of the house was built in the 1700s. It will be so fun."

"I'm not sure if fun is the right word. It truly isn't all that impressive."

"But I would love to find inventive ways to keep you warm at night," she said as he let her hand drift up Graham's leg until it was less than an inch away from his cock.

He looked at her and raised an eyebrow.

"Are ye looking for a repeat of last night?"

"That and more . . . if you are up to it," she said, sliding her hand up that last inch, his cock twitching to life beneath it.

"More than up to it, mo ghrádh," he said as he raised his hips up into her hand before kissing her. Her stomach grumbled, and he chuckled. "Let's come back to this in a moment. First, it sounds like we should put some food in yer belly."

"Well . . . it is the day after Thanksgiving. So, you know what that means?" she asked.

He looked at her, waiting for the answer.

"That means pie for breakfast."

After they had pie for breakfast and some leftover turkey, Graham went to work, clearing about three feet of snow on his way to the barn. His winters had been snowy all his life, but he had never seen that much snow. He dug out a path to the stable. It was cold but plenty warm for horses to stay warm in the stable.

Graham came back into the house and stomped the snow from his boots. Hannah was curled up on the couch with a blanket, reading a book. She was warm, drinking the tea. The sight stirred something in his heart. This woman was warm and content, and it was because of what he had done.

After he had slipped his boots off and hung his coat on the hook by the door, he went over and sat with her on the couch.

"What are ye reading?" he asked.

She showed him a blue book with gold lettering that read *Outlander*.

"*Outlander*. I found this on the shelf. My mom used to love these books. It's interesting to me right now."

"Why is that?"

"Because it is a love story about a woman from the 1940s who time travels and finds herself in the Scottish Highlands in the 1740s."

"Aye, that is interesting. Is it any good?"

"Yeah, there is a whole show based on these books. It's a popular series."

"May I?" Graham asked as he held his hand out for the book.

He inspected the well-loved book. Books in his day and age were something very different. He grew up with a library in his house, and he loved to read the books. But most households in his time didn't have books, let alone a room full of them, and even knowing how to read was a privilege. He handed the book back to her.

"Read it to me," he said.

"You know how to read."

"Aye, I do, but I like yer voice and what else have we to do? The fire is burning, the horses are tended to, there is plenty of wood cut."

"Okay," she said.

For the rest of the day, she read to him. He made a stew for dinner over the fire, and for dessert, they made s'mores. Except for a text to let her mother know they were safe, Hannah stayed off her phone, and all the other modern conveniences.

She continued to read to Graham well into the evening. The part in the book, when the two main characters, Claire and Jamie, got married, came as a shock to him. The writing was quite explicit. Graham thought it was downright indecent, but he had learned to keep those thoughts to himself.

He also couldn't help but feel a little turned on as those words came out of Hannah's mouth. At first, she seemed uncomfortable speaking them, then she found her rhythm again, and the words danced off her tongue. Graham's cock twitched as she spoke the words.

She lay on the couch with her feet in Graham's lap. He rubbed her feet, listening. He looked over at her and slowly started moving his hands up her legs.

When he had his hand resting on her inner thigh, she stopped, looked at him, and cocked her eyebrow.

"What is it you are doing with your hand, Mr. MacNeil?" she asked in a proper tone.

"I think ye ken what I am doing with my hand, Mistress Glenn," he said, inching his hand higher.

Then Hannah put the book down, and Graham moved over to her. He grabbed her legs and yanked, pulling her flat on her back on the couch.

Hannah giggled. Something about this usually serious

woman giggling made Graham's heart sing. He maneuvered himself between her legs.

"I think I am done with reading for the night," he whispered in her ear. Then he let his tongue trace along the edge of her ear.

"Well, what are we to do, then?" she said with an overly innocent tone and batted her eye lashes.

Graham bent down and kissed her deeply, claiming her mouth. He felt like Hannah was his, like she belonged to him, body and soul. After the night before and the power outage, his confidence had returned. He felt like he was finally getting his footing. He kissed her deep and ground his hard cock against her sex. She moaned into his kiss.

They made love in front of the fire. All night. They allowed themselves pleasure in each other's body. Graham took her again and again. He would never have his fill of this woman. Being inside of her was like breathing; it gave him life. The dynamic between them was changing, and Graham welcomed it. He wanted nothing but to make this woman happy all day, then slide into her every night.

Maybe he had died, and she was his own personal heaven. That made as much sense as the truth that existed between them. Whatever it was, he was going to keep it that way.

CHAPTER 21

*C*hristmas was quickly approaching, and Hannah was in prep mode. Once again, her whole family was coming to the farmhouse to celebrate. She hadn't spoken to her family since they had missed Thanksgiving and hadn't spoken to her dad since the dinner after game day.

In fact, they hadn't really talked to anyone. She and Graham had been cocooned in their perfect little bubble. Their perfect little sex-filled bubble.

During the day, Hannah busied herself writing her first novel. Graham did chores around the farm and helped Sam with upgrades to the orchard. There had been the occasional outing to their favorite karaoke bar with Poppy and Sam, but most nights, they would spend at home.

They would curl up and watch movies, or they would take turns reading to each other, but they would always end up in bed together. Hannah had never been with anyone like Graham in bed. From the first time they had sex, he took control and rocked her world. For someone like Hannah, letting go of control was hard. She had never trusted someone enough to let them completely control the situation, but she felt so safe and adored by him that it felt natural.

She was so impressed by him. For someone who had only been there for three months' time, he was by far the most self-efficient and helpful person Hannah had ever been with. Hannah was trying to rein in her emotions because she knew she was falling in love with him, and it was a love she had never felt before. Saying goodbye in March was going to be the hardest thing she had ever done, but she didn't really see a way around it. He didn't belong here.

"Hannah, What about this one?" Graham called to her.

"No, bigger!" she called back.

They walked through the woods, searching for the perfect Christmas tree.

"I can't believe we are going to cut down a perfectly good tree and put it in the house."

"We do it every year and then, in spring, we plant two new ones. It is a family tradition," Hannah said as she caught up to Graham before slipping her mitten'd hand into his. "At least some of the snow has melted, so we could come out and get one."

Graham kissed her on the head.

"Aye, whatever pleases ye, mo ghrádh."

They walked hand in hand. The woods around the farm were still snowy, and the snow crunched under their boots. Hannah's round cheeks were red with cold, but just being near him, she didn't feel cold.

Then she spied it. The perfect tree.

"That one! Let's get that one," she said as she came up to a seven-foot spruce tree.

"This is the one?" Graham eyed the tree.

"Yes!" Hannah said, clapping her hands, giddy.

"All right, lass, let me chop down this perfectly good tree to bring into the house."

"It is appreciated," she said, smiling up at him.

"How much?" he asked with a glint in his eye.

Hannah gave him a coy smile. "I'll show you later."

After they had shaken all the snow out of the tree, they got it set up in the house. Hannah showed Graham how to help put on the lights. The rest of the ornaments would wait until the next day, when her family would arrive. Hannah had just changed into pajamas and was getting ready to relax on the couch with Graham, which had quickly become her favorite part of the day.

As she sat on to the couch next to Graham, he put a little box in her lap.

"What's this?" she asked.

"I thought I would give ye yer gift tonight before yer family arrives tomorrow."

She untied the bow and opened the little box. Inside was a necklace, a beautiful silver chain brandishing a beautiful sapphire pendant. It was breathtaking.

"Graham. This is beautiful. Where did you get this?"

"I brought it with me. I carry that in my sporran. It belonged to my mother, and I always told myself I would give it to the first woman I ever loved."

Hannah lifted the necklace with trembling hands. Not only was this the most beautiful gift she had ever been given, but unless she had just hallucinated, Graham just said he loved her.

"What?"

"It was my mother's."

"Graham, don't you want to save this for whoever you end up marrying? I can't keep this."

"Hannah Glenn, are ye refusin' my gift?"

"No, I just don't want you to regret giving it to me . . . when you . . . ya know, have to go back."

That was another thing that they had stopped discussing

in the lovely sex-filled cocoon. The fact that he was leaving in a few months' time, and all of it would have been a mere magical memory. He took the necklace and placed it on Hannah's neck.

"No, I won't regret it. I am giving it to you because I love you."

"You love me?"

"Of course I do, ye daft thing. Did ye think I just go around beddin' women I dinna care for deeply?"

"Well, I know, but I just didn't expect . . ."

"Hannah," he said gently. His hand lifted her chin. "If we belonged to each other's time, this gift would be accompanied with a wedding proposal. In my time, I would have wed you a long time ago. Right after I punched that fellow at the wedding and kissed ye. But in this time, I would propose to ye tonight. But seeing as we do not belong, I can only think to give you this. You are my love, Hannah, now and always."

Before Hannah could stop them, tears streamed down her face. She loved him, too, and she knew it. She loved him more than she had ever loved anyone in her entire life. Graham wiped away her tears.

"Hush now, dinna fash, mo ghrádh. I just wanted to tell ye what ye mean to me. If ye dinna feel the same, it is all right."

"Graham, it's not that. I love you, too. More than you know . . . I don't actually have a gift for you, but I want to share with you what I've been writing if you want to hear it."

"Of course, I do."

Hannah got off the couch and went and got her laptop. She returned to the couch and opened it. She took a breath.

"Okay, I will read it to you."

She started reading her story. It was a story about a woman who woke up one morning to find a time-traveling highlander in her barn. At first, they fought all the time. She thought he was a brute, and he thought she was an uppity woman in a time he didn't understand, but they were undeniably attracted to each other. And soon, they could no longer deny those feelings and fell desperately in love with each other.

By the end, Hannah was wiping away tears from her eyes as she read it. She even caught Graham rubbing his eyes, too, but she would never say anything, because although he was probably the most forward-thinking man from the 1740s, he was still a prideful Scotsman.

When she finished reading, she closed her laptop.

"Well, that's what I got so far . . . so, you see, Graham MacNeil, I love you, too."

"You wrote our story?" His voice sounded raspy and filled with emotion.

"I did. I couldn't think of a better love story."

"That's because there isn't one."

Hannah had been fighting this feeling, but there was no more fighting it. She was hopelessly in love with this man, who was leaving. She didn't want him to leave. Maybe he could just stay there. But surely, he wanted to go back to his own time. He had a life before her, he would have a life after her. Maybe he was just there to help her grow. Whatever the reason for this magical happenstance, she would be forever grateful for the winter she got to spend with her highlander.

THE NEXT DAY, Hannah fretted around, making sure everything was ready for her family to come in. Graham was sleeping in the barn, which Hannah hated, but he flat out refused to sleep in the same bed with her under the same roof as her parents. Hannah tried to explain that it would be fine, but he said it would not be fine for him. So, he was in the office in the barn, which was heated but not all that warm and definitely not cozy, but it was the way he wanted it.

Hannah's brother and his family were the first ones to arrive and unpack upstairs. The kids were out in the barn with Graham when her parents pulled up. They had picked up Josie from the airport. Hannah had been on the phone with her mom a lot that week, planning all the details of Christmas, but Hannah still hadn't talked to her father. She had never gone that long without talking to him.

Hannah heard her parents' car pull up. Josie was the first one in the kitchen.

"Hi, Han!" she called as she wrapped Hannah into a hug. "Merry Christmas! How are things going here at the farm? Do you miss the city yet?"

"Surprisingly, not even a little," she said.

"I saw Graham heading up to help with the bags. So are you guys . . . ya know." She inserted her index finger into her other hand that formed a circle, pumping her finger repeatedly.

"Josie!" Hannah scoffed and batted at her hands. "I don't know what you're talking about."

"Yes, you do, are you and Graham doin—"

"Did I just hear my name?" Graham asked, as he came through the door, carrying four bags like a pack mule.

"You did! I was just asking Hannah if she ever acted on her little crush she has on you."

Hannah shot daggers at her sister.

"Aye, she did. And the fondness is mutual," he said with his easy nature and kissed Hannah on top of her head as he took the bags upstairs.

"Hannah, did that man just kiss your head?" her mother squawked with surprise.

Hannah turned to see her mother standing in the doorway with a confused look on her face.

"Ummm . . . yeah, Mom. Graham, and I are kind of dating."

"Really?" she said in a perplexed tone.

"Yeah . . . it just kind of happened."

"He's very attractive," her mother continued.

"I know." said Hannah, unsure of what to say.

"And you guys are together?"

Hannah connected the dots. Her mother was shocked that someone who is so undeniably handsome would date someone fat. Hannah tried not to be offended—her mother's worth was still so much tied up in the diet industry bullshit, that she didn't think someone who looked like Hannah belonged with someone who looked like Graham. He should be with someone who looked like her sister. Hannah reminded herself it was just her mother's trauma speaking and had nothing to do with Hannah or Graham.

"Who's together?" Hannah's father said as he walked through the door.

"Hannah and Graham," Josie said in a sing-songy voice.

"Would you shut up? We are not twelve."

"Are you dating my daughter, son?" her father said to Graham as he walked down the stairs.

"With your permission, sir. Yes. I very much like spending time with yer daughter," Graham said, his tone firm.

"Well, I think we will need to have a little chat later."

"Yes, sir. I would like that very much."

What is even happening? Her dad didn't talk like this to her other boyfriends. Why were they talking about her like she was a maiden with a dowry?

"Oh, for fuck's sake!" Hannah called out just as Bailey and Braxton ran through the kitchen. They both stopped and gasped at Hannah.

"Aunt Hannah said a bad word!" Bailey said.

"Yeah, F is a really bad word." Braxton agreed.

And just like that, Hannah and Graham were officially out of the wonderful, cozy, sex-filled cocoon and fully immersed in family nonsense.

"I know . . . don't say words like me," she said before turning to her family. "But for the love of god, can we please move on? I am a grown ass woman who has brought home men before. Everything is fine."

"Aye, so I'm nothin' special, then?" Graham winked at her, and she wanted to swoon and scream at the same time.

"Aunt Hannah said another bad word!" Bailey said.

"Your Aunt Hannah has a potty mouth, doesn't she?" Joanne said to the kids as she escorted them into the living room.

Josie and Richard headed upstairs, leaving Hannah and Graham alone in the kitchen.

He walked over to her and pulled her close. It was like he could feel the tension radiating off her, and his closeness brought her calm.

"Mo ghrádh, you need to breathe. You are wound so tight you're bound to snap. Everything will be all right."

She took a deep breath and leaned into him. He was right. With him there, she would be fine.

As the visit went on, things remained good. On Christmas Eve, they all had a lovely dinner and decorated the tree, one of Hannah's favorite family traditions. Game day could go to hell, but this was lovely. They set out the cookies for Santa and some carrots for the reindeer. Graham was enjoying the novelty of Christmas.

Christmas morning came, lively with presents, brunch, and board games, but not Monopoly. Never Monopoly after the battle of 2009.

The best sledding hill on the property was shady, and

there was still plenty of snow, so Graham and Brett took the kids sledding. It was a picture-perfect Christmas. After the awkward beginning to the weekend—when they all found out Hannah was dating Graham—everything since was fine. He fit right in, and things could not have been better. Even things with Hannah's dad had been okay—strained but okay. It was a definite step in the right direction.

After the weekend, everyone packed up to head home. Brett and his family had left. Joanne, Richard, and Josie were leaving to take Josie to the airport in a couple of hours from that point. Hannah was walking past her dad's office when he called her in.

"Hannah, just the person I was looking for. Will you come in here for a moment?"

"Yeah, Dad. What's up?"

Hannah walked into the office and saw her dad on a call with someone.

"Come over here, Hannah. I have someone I want to introduce you to."

Hannah walked around her dad's desk and joined him. She looked at the computer screen. Smiling back at her was the face of Lucy Chen.

Lucy Chen ran a highly successful law firm in the city, who worked for environmental justice and had won some big cases.

"Oh my god! Lucy Chen!"

"Hi, Hannah. Your father has been telling me about you."

Richard smiled at his daughter. "I met Ms. Chen at a conference in November. I mentioned my brilliant daughter, and I thought you two might like to chat."

"Oh, umm, yeah, that's great. I am such a supporter of the work you do, Ms. Chen."

"Well, I will just let you two chat," Richard said as he

stood to leave. "Have a seat. I'm sure you two have a lot to talk about."

Hannah looked at Richard suspiciously.

"Thanks, Dad," she said as she watched Richard walk out of the room.

"Hannah, your father was telling me what good work you did at Glass and Associates."

"Thank you. I was there for a couple years. I learned a lot."

"Your father also told me you are looking for a change of pace. We are about to take on a big oil company, and I have been looking at your resume. I think you would be a great addition to our team."

"My resume? I'm sorry. I don't understand."

"Look, just between us, I know that Roger Glass is an ass. I would hate to see a promising young attorney like yourself leave the field because of him. I know you would thrive here. After speaking with your father and Sadie from over at the Glass office, I would like to officially offer you a job as an attorney with our firm. I will send the paperwork over to you. Let me know when you decide. I will be back in the office the second week of January."

"You're offering me a job?"

"That's the gist of it. We would love to take you on and see if you are a good fit. We could use someone with your skills. Not to mention, you've been working on the other side of corporate law for a while. I'm sure you're sharp on how to deal with them. I hear you were very good and a hard worker but didn't really like what you did."

"That's correct."

"Okay, then, just email me back when you make your decision. We will get everything ironed out and join the team in January."

"Okay, thank you."

"It was very nice to talk to you Hannah, I look forward to hearing from you."

"Thank you so much. This really is a great opportunity. I will think it over."

Hannah shut the laptop. What the hell just happened?! She had a range of emotions.

One, she had just Facetimed with Lucy Chen. Lucy Chen had been one of Hannah's role models in the field since law school. In fact, she interviewed there when she was looking for a job and would have worked there for less than she was making at Glass & Associates, but it just didn't work out. Two, she couldn't help feeling like she had just been set up. Her dad went behind her back and got her a job. She was furious, but how could anyone be furious about that? When someone does something nice for you, something you used to dream about, how could you be mad? She walked out of the room and into the kitchen. She saw her dad getting his coat on.

"What the hell was that?"

"I thought you would be pleased. I know you look up to Ms. Chen."

"I do, but I told you I didn't want to be a lawyer anymore."

"Look, Banana, I know Roger is an ass, and I know that isn't the kind of law you want to be practicing, and since you won't come and work for me, I thought it would be a good opportunity for your career."

"Dad. You are not listening to me. I do not want to be a lawyer. I'm not sure I ever really did."

"That's nonsense, Hannah, all that work in law school, graduating top of your class. You are good at this. Now you can be one of the good guys. I think you will really like it if you give it a chance."

"Why aren't you listening to me? I don't want to do it."

"What are you going to do? Sit up here, playing house

with your boyfriend forever? That's just not feasible. How will you provide for yourself? And if I'm not mistaken, isn't Graham going back to Scotland in March? This was a break, Hannah, and we all need them, but I think it is time to get back to the real world."

Those words might as well have been a slap across her face.

"Dad, I will figure it out. Please trust me."

He took a breath and looked her in the eye. He gave his head a little nod. "I do trust you, but please just think about this. It's the real world, Hannah. I have always been able to count on you. Just give it a chance."

"Fine. I need some air." She pushed past him and got to the door.

She heard her mother and Josie coming down the stairs.

"Well, that's everything. We need to hit the road to make it to the airport," her mother said. She turned and gave Hannah a big hug.

"It was so good to see you, sweetheart. Let us know when you are back in the city. We will take you out for dinner."

"Thanks, Mom," she said.

"Catch ya later, sis," Josie said, giving Hannah a hug.

They all said their goodbyes, and Hannah watched them drive away. She was still so angry. She couldn't decide if she was mad because he went behind her back or maybe that a small portion of her thought he might be right. Maybe she was just living in a fantasy world. Maybe Graham didn't want to stay there with her, so what would she do?

She needed to find Graham. They needed to talk about this.

She was hoping they could find a way to get back in their little cocoon. She wanted the bubble back. She pulled her jacket on and walked down to the barn. The door was open, so she slipped inside. She could hear Graham in the office, who did not sound happy.

"Ock!" Graham cried out, followed by a string of Gaelic she didn't understand. "I just canna understand this blasted time. I canna wait to get back to my own."

Hannah gasped and reached for the wall.

In one moment, it all came crumbling down around her. Her dad was right. This was all a dream. She was not living in the real world. Graham was leaving in less than three months. Hannah had fooled herself into thinking this could last forever, but he never said he intended to stay. And it was clear he didn't want to. Hannah had just assumed that he would. How could she have been so wrong?

Tears rolled down her face. She had to get out of there before he saw her like that. She needed to pull it together. She slipped out of the barn and made her way back to the house.

She went to her laptop and checked her email. At the top was an email from Lucy Chen's office with an official job offer. Hannah opened it. It was more money that she was making at her old job. She respected the person she would be working for. She would be doing good work. This was the opportunity of a lifetime. And her life there wasn't real. Graham would leave, and she would be brokenhearted and alone. The thought of that made her sob.

This looks like an amazing opportunity. I am excited to accept your offer. I am available to start after the first of the year. I look forward to our work together.

Hannah Glenn

She took a breath and hit send.

Then she decided she would take a shower until she was done crying and could face Graham if the hot water would hold out long enough.

CHAPTER 22

*G*raham had been enjoying the holiday with Hannah and her family. He could see the anxiety in Hannah when she was around her family. He wished more than anything he could help her with that. He loved the Hannah he got to see and spend time with. And from what he could tell, the only people who really got to see that version of Hannah were him and Poppy.

He counted himself lucky to be one of the people close to her, but he wished more people could see how amazing she was when she was relaxed. She was funny and caring. He wagered those were things most people would not describe her as, but they were at the top of his list—that and damn sexy.

Things with Hannah's family were easy. Hannah's mother seemed to like him, along with her sister and brother. Graham was most concerned about Hannah's father because Hannah seemed keen on having his approval. She seemed to miss it for herself, so if he could make him see that he and Hannah could have a life here, that he could find a way to provide for her, maybe Hannah would feel a little better.

He hadn't talked to Hannah about it yet, but he was thinking about staying there with her. He missed his home, but after his father died and after having joined the rebellion, there wasn't much joy for him there. He loved Scotland and would gladly die for the cause, but he had Hannah to think about. He was so deeply in love with her, and she seemed to feel the same way.

Graham had been talking with Sam about some things. The Smith Family Orchard was a staple in the community. Graham had been talking to him about ways he could help. He knew how to work the land because he grew up on the farm. Sam was talking about branching out into other things to sell things like eggs and cheese. Graham could help with that. Graham also knew how to raise animals, and Sam had been wanting to add a petting zoo, but he didn't have experience with animals. Graham mentioned to Mr. Glenn that he and Sam had been working on some ideas for the land.

"Wonderful, we have lots of land. Might as well put it to good use. Why don't you send me your ideas, and I will have a look?" he said.

"Aye, should I send them in the mail?" asked Graham.

Richard gave a belly laugh.

"You are a funny one, Graham. No, my email will do just fine." He reached into his pocket, pulled out a business card, and handed it to Graham.

"Thank you, sir."

Graham got to work to figure out how to send Mr. Glenn his ideas. There was an old computer in the office in the stable. Sam had shown him how to order feed and some other bookkeeping, but he hadn't touched it since. It wasn't a point of pride anymore. If he was going to belong in this time, he needed to learn how to do things like this. He watched Hannah on her laptop, and she made it look easy. He was going to figure this out.

He pulled up a chair up to the desk and looked at the ancient desktop sitting on the desk. First, he tapped on the screen. Hannah's phone seemed to work that way, but nothing happened. Then he saw a little button. He pushed it, and the screen turned on. After showing nothing but a moving circle for a few minutes, it looked like a screen he remembered, but he had no idea what to do next. He attempted to touch the screen one more time.

"Oh, Christ, there has to be an easier way."

He took a deep breath and tried again to figure it out. He wiped his hand down his face. If he truly belonged in that timeline, and if he deserved a chance to be a part of Hannah's life, it was something he was going to need to figure out. Then he recalled Sam moving the little thing on the table around. He moved it, and a little arrow popped up.

"There's a start," he said as he moved the little arrow all over the screen. He could feel the frustration growing.

"Ock! I dinna ken what to do next," he said, repeatedly picking up the mouse and thumping it back down again.

Then he looked at the letters on the keyboard, which seemed to be in no particular order. He pecked out M-A-I-L and looked at the screen, hopeful, but nothing happened. He muttered to himself, trying to quiet the frustration boiling up inside him. He pushed buttons. He moved the little arrow. He touched the screen again, but nothing seemed to work. He was going to have to ask Hannah or Sam for help. His pride was roaring inside of him. He stood and slammed the chair back under the desk.

"Ock!" Graham cried out, "I just canna understand this blasted time. I canna wait to get back to my own."

As those words came out, Graham knew they weren't true. He wanted to stay there, but he didn't know how to do anything. He decided to take one of the horses for a ride and blow off some steam before he humbled himself to ask Hannah for help.

By the time he was done riding and had the horse in the stable, the family had all cleared out. He was eager to get inside and have Hannah all to himself once more. He made his way up to the house, and he couldn't find her. He heard the shower running, so he decided to sit down and read from the book Hannah had been reading to him.

After a while, he heard the shower turn off and heard Hannah go into her room. The thought of her naked and wet in there had his cock pushing against his pants. He pushed that thought away. She had probably needed to unwind after all that time with her family . . . *Although, it is a truly exceptional way to unwind. No!* he told himself. *Only if she wants.*

When Hannah finally came down the stairs, he could guess it was probably the last thing on her mind. She sat on the couch—on the other side of it—tucking her feet up under herself before reaching for the remote.

Graham reached out and gave her foot a gentle wiggle. "Why so far away?"

"I'm just tired," she answered back without glancing his way.

They sat in silence, with Graham reading the book and Hannah watching TV. Graham could feel the distance, but he was giving her space. The clock ticked on, and dinner time came rolling around.

"Mo ghrádh, it is getting late. Are you hungry?"

"Not really. I will probably just eat some leftovers later."

"Would you like me to fix ye some food?" he asked.

"No, I'm fine, but if you are hungry, go ahead and eat."

Graham was starting to worry something was wrong. He pushed those thoughts away. Maybe she was always like this when her family left? Maybe she was sad? He was trying to figure it out. Last time they had left, they were not spending time together like this, and she was injured, so he had nothing to compare it to.

"Is everything all right? You seem like something's worryin' ye lass"

"No, Graham. I'm fine. I'm just tired." She reached out and squeezed his hand. She looked away quickly, but her eyes looked red and glassy, like she had been crying. He had a feeling that "fine" in this case didn't actually mean fine, but if she was not ready to talk, he would give her space.

He got up and fixed them both a plate of food and brought it to her. She looked up at him with tears in her eyes.

"Hannah, for the love of Christ, what is wrong? Have I done something to upset ye?"

"No, not at all," she said, shaking her head as she swallowed the tears. "Thanks for this."

He nodded, took his place on the couch, and watched the show with her.

When she was finished, she turned to Graham. "I think I am just going to go to bed. I think I might be coming down with a cold."

"Would you like me to come with ye?"

"No, that's okay. It's so early. Why don't you just stay here? Come to bed when you are ready." She got up and took her plate to the kitchen.

"Good night, Graham," she said and disappeared up the stairs, without a kiss good night.

Something had happened—only he didn't know what.

THE NEXT MORNING, he woke up with a stiff neck. He had slept on the couch. This situation with Hannah was uncharted territory, and he wasn't sure how to act. She was in the kitchen, making coffee.

"Good morning, mo ghrádh, are you feeling well today?"

"Yep, must have slept it off. Poppy has the day off. I think I am going to go spend the day with her. We haven't spent as much time together as we normally do. I miss her."

"Of course, I will see ye when ye return home."

"Yep, sounds good . . . well, I'm going to get ready to go."

And at that, she disappeared up the stairs. Graham's mind was reeling. After the night before and then the following morning, he was trying to puzzle out what had happened. What had gone wrong? What had her acting in such a way? Did she not want him anymore? He put that thought way far down in the back of his mind. He couldn't think that. She had changed his whole life, and he was certain she was fond of him. Things had gone well with her family. He just couldn't figure it out. She came back down the stairs, dressed and ready to go. He reached out and took her hand, and she looked at him. Her eyes were still glassy and far away.

"Bye, Graham. I will see you tonight."

Then she slipped out the door.

Graham was lost, feeling that way for the first time since he'd been there. Sure, at first, he felt very lost, but in a fish-out-of-water kind of way. This felt like heartbreak, and he had no idea why. He headed to the stable and thought mucking about in there and going for a long ride might do him some good, even if it was freezing out. He was being iced out inside, too.

That night, when Hannah came home, he was praying she would talk to him. He heard the car pull up. Hannah walked in, and she looked terrible.

"Graham, I think we need to talk."

"Aye, I think we do. What is wrong?" he said.

He walked over to her, and she fell into his arms, crying. He held her until she stopped. She took his hand and walked him over to the couch. He wasn't quite sure why the walk to the couch felt like a walk to the noose, but it sure did.

"I have been offered a job. It is a really good job working for a woman I have idolized since law school."

"All right, that doesn't sound worth tears." He gently wiped the remaining tears from her face.

"It is in the city. It starts in a week."

Graham's heart dropped out of his chest. There it was. The reason she had been so upset. She was leaving and didn't know how to tell him.

"I know you can't live in the city, but I mean this isn't forever, right? This always had an end date. I can't put my life on hold and pass up this opportunity."

"No, ye cannot."

"I'm just s-s-s-sad," she sniffed out, crying again, hiding her face in her hands.

Graham's heart was breaking in two looking at her like that, but she was right. He had hoped to stay, but maybe it wasn't for the best. It didn't seem to be what she wanted.

"Dinna fash," he said, pulling her into an embrace.

He held her for a long time while she wept on his shoulder, wiping away a few stray tears of his own.

That night, they just held each other. They eventually turned on a show and snuggled close on the couch. They went up to bed and held each other as they fell asleep; neither of them could bring themselves to talk about what was to come.

The next day, they woke up to a somber feeling. They tried to keep it together and make breakfast together like they used to, but the ease of their once-perfect in sync dynamic was gone. Later that night, Hannah looked at him.

"Thank you for everything, Graham. You are an amazing person, and you are going to make a lucky lady really happy back in the 1740s."

"You, Hannah Glenn, are a truly remarkable woman. You have made me a better man."

"I think I should move back into the city. I haven't been in my apartment since September, so I probably have some work to do there before I start my new job."

"Aye, I understand. Ye must get ready."

"Yeah, but you should totally stay in the house and everything. I know Sam still wants to finish whatever projects you guys are working on. You guys are friends, right? So, you won't be totally alone. I just think it is for the best. Rip the Band-Aid off."

"Aye, I'm not sure what that last bit means, but I get the gist. Is that what ye think is best?"

"Yes," she said as her voice hitched. "I think I need to leave. It is just too hard."

Graham's shoulders slumped, and his head fell. There was nothing he could say. He reached out and squeezed her hand.

"Sam and Jackson's wedding is the day before the equinox. I will come back for the wedding and then we can get you back where you belong."

Those words, "where you belong," echoed around in Graham's head. He had started to feel like he belonged there, with Hannah, but who was he kidding? He needed to go back. Back to his uncle, back to the rebellion, where he belonged. He looked at Hannah and nodded.

"But maybe you'll be my date for the wedding?" she asked timidly.

"It would be my honor, Hannah Glenn, to accompany ye to a wedding unlike any I will ever see again," he said with a smile.

Her soft chuckle didn't fully bubble up, the weight between them bogging it down.

"So, I think I am going to go back to the city in the morning. Poppy is going to drop me off at the train station . . . . But tonight, will you sleep with me? Just sleep. I just want to feel your arms around me for one last night."

"Of course, it would please me very much. I will miss this soft round arse of yers. Ye really know how to keep a fellow warm," he said, trying to make her laugh.

She smiled at him and gave his shoulder a gentle shove. He took hold of her hand and pulled her into a hug.

"Ye truly are one of a kind, Hannah Glenn. I hope ye ken that. Good things are going to come yer way, of that I am certain."

"Why did you have to be so perfect?" She laughed, wiping away a tear. "Can't you be a brutish over-bearing Scotsman again? The one I can't wait to send back in time."

"Aye, I will aim to displease ye," he said with a grin.

And that broke the tension. She laughed fully and smiled at him.

"This sucks," she said.

"Aye, it does."

CHAPTER 23

Hannah and Graham said their goodbyes and tried to hold it together, but when Hannah walked to Poppy's car, she had tears streaming down her face. She threw her bag in the back seat and climbed in next to Poppy. She looked over at Hannah, her eyes clouded with concern.

"Tell me again why you're doing this," she said.

"Please, just drive." Hannah looked lifelessly out the window.

Poppy nodded and gave Hannah's hand a squeeze. They pulled out of the driveway. The ride to the train station was silent. Hannah couldn't bring herself to say anything. She just sat there silently, weeping. Why did he have to be so amazing? He didn't belong there, and he had a whole life to go back to. He had loved ones and things he cared about. Of course he wanted to go back. She had thought he loved her enough to stay, but sometimes, love isn't enough. This was, apparently, one of those times. As much as Hannah hated to admit it, her dad was right. It was just a dream, and it was time to get back to reality.

Poppy parked the car and turned off the engine. She turned to look at Hannah.

"Why are you doing this?"

"You know why. He is leaving. Then what? I am just heartbroken in that big house all alone. At least now I'm heartbroken with a good job. I have wanted to work for Lucy Chen since law school. This is a great opportunity. It was going to end sometime . . . so the time is now."

"But why? You love him, he loves you. I have seen how you two are with each other. There is something there."

"Yeah . . ." Hannah sniffed. "There is, but that doesn't change that he is leaving, and long distance isn't really an option here, you know that."

"Why don't you ask him to stay?"

"Because he wants to go back."

"He told you that?"

"No, but I overheard him talking in the barn about how much he hated it here and how much he wants to go back to his own time."

Poppy shook her head in protest.

"Yeah, that's throwing me, Hannah, for real. I think you need to talk to him."

"Poppy. I can't pass up this opportunity, and . . . it just hurts too much," she said with renewed tears streaming down her face again.

"Okay," Poppy said. "I won't bring it up again. I'm here for you. You know that," she said as she reached over and gave her friend a long hug. Hannah held on and cried.

IT HAD BEEN OVER A WEEK. Hannah had texted Graham when she got to the city that she was safe. She was surprised when he texted her back. He hated the phone she had gotten for him. He could never figure it out, but it was nice to hear from him. That was the last time they had talked.

Hannah had tried to busy herself by getting ready for her new job and getting her apartment back in order. She went grocery shopping and did some cleaning. She was going to lunch with Sadie to talk about the new job. She was trying to get back to city life, like a giant highlander-sized hole in her heart didn't exist.

Hannah: Hey I'm back in town let's do lunch.

Sadie: Yes! Wanna meet up at Pete's for lunch next week?

WALKING INTO A BROOKLYN RESTAURANT, Hannah looked for Sadie. It was her first time seeing Sadie since her wedding, since everything had changed when she left the city the first time.

She found her at a table in the back. She was sitting there with her husband, who was the chef. He got up from the table and bent down and gave Sadie a quick kiss. It was a small reflexive kiss, but something about it pulled at Hannah's heart. She shook her head, steeled herself, and walked over.

Sadie turned and beamed at her. Her inky-black ringlets tied up in a colorful scarf, and she wore a simple black shirt and jeans. She was stunning. She and Hannah always looked to be opposite of each other physically, but their personalities were similar. She needed Sadie to tell her she did the right thing. Sadie had always been as career-driven and no nonsense as she was.

"Hey, lady," she said. She stood and gave Hannah a hug. "I'm glad you are back in town. We have a lot to catch up on."

"I know. It's been too long. How are you doing?"

"I'm good, still working for Roger, but I am starting to

look elsewhere. It just isn't the same without you. How is Lucy Chen?"

"I've only been there a week, but so far so good."

"So, tell me about life on the farm. How was your break from the city?" she asked.

Hannah took a moment. She was waiting for talking about that to be less painful, but she had no idea how long that would take. Luckily, just then, Peter, Sadie's partner, brought out soup. That was the thing about being friends with the chef—he always just brought out what he felt like. That day, it looked like they were starting with butternut squash soup.

"It was good," she managed to say. Stirring her soup, she looked up at Sadie, who was looking at her with her eyebrow raised.

"What are you not telling me? You are back in town with your dream job, but you don't seem very happy about it. Does this have anything to do with the Scottish hottie you brought to my wedding?"

"I never apologized for what happened at the wedding—"

"Please, no need. That guy needed to be punched for years. I'm glad someone actually did it. It made the day more memorable."

"Still, I'm sorry."

"What's up with that guy? Are you still together?"

Hannah looked back at her soup.

"What happened?" she asked. "Do I need to make a trip to the country? You can take the girl out of the Bronx, but you can't take the Bronx out of the girl." She reached for her hoop earrings.

"No, nothing like that. Things just didn't work out timing-wise. He is going back to Scotland in March, and I got this offer. It was time."

"Why do I feel like there is something you are not telling me?"

"No, really, that's about it. It sucks because he is hands down the best guy I have ever dated, but, ya know, the timing and all."

"I know long distance sucks, but maybe you guys could make something work."

"Are you, the only person who may have put in more hours than me, telling me that a long-distance relationship would actually work?"

"Hey, girl, I'm as surprised as you are, but if he makes you happy, I say find a way."

Hannah's eyes burned. She thought she had cried all the tears she had to cry, but more threatened to spill down her cheeks. She blinked them away.

"Things aren't quite that cut-and-dry with us." Her voice cracked on the last word.

"Hey, now"—Sadie reached across the table and squeezed her hand—"what's this all about? This is the first time I have ever seen you in knots over a guy. You usually just kick 'em to the curb when they piss you off one too many times."

Hannah wiped away the one tear that had managed to escape.

"Things with Graham are different. We had a good thing. I didn't even think I was going to come back here. I was going to stop being a lawyer and live in the country with him but then this opportunity happened with Lucy Chen, and Graham is still leaving, so here I am."

"Good sex, huh?" Sadie joked.

"Hands down best sex of my life," Hannah said without stopping to think.

"Damn, girl." She grinned at her. "Look, I don't know what happened, but I know you looked pretty happy at the wedding. He jacked a guy in the face to defend your honor, and now you're telling me it was the best sex of your life. Dream job or not, you guys need to figure it out."

"Who are you, and what have you done with Sadie?" Hannah asked.

"I know. Love has made me soft," she said with a shake of her head.

And, as if on cue, Peter brought out two plates of salmon and set them down in front of them. He slid in next to Sadie and joined them.

"How are you doing, Hannah? I haven't talked to you in ages. I don't think I've seen you since your date punched someone at our wedding." He grinned at her.

Hannah put her head in her hands and groaned.

"Don't worry, we loved it. It's a good wedding story. Glad to have you back in the city, though. I'm sure I will be seeing you around." He patted her on the shoulder. He stood and gave Sadie a quick kiss. "I gotta get back to work."

"All right, we talked about your Scottish predicament. I say don't let it go if you aren't ready, but you clearly are ready for a subject change. So, how is Lucy Chen? Are you guys really taking on E&G oil?"

Happy for the subject change, they spent the rest of their lunch catching up on office drama, talking about Hannah's new job and about new job prospects for Sadie. It was a much-needed distraction.

CHAPTER 24

*T*he day Hannah left, Graham couldn't hold it together. He cried like he had the day his mother died when he was twelve. It felt like he had lost part of his own heart when she walked out. He wanted to stay with her, but she had said it herself: he didn't belong here. It was not his time. He must go home to Scotland and the rebellion.

Later that night, he heard a knock at the door. He opened it and saw Sam, who was holding pizza and a six-pack.

"I thought you might like company. Poppy told me Hannah went back to the city today."

"Thank ye," Graham said, opening the door to him. It was a welcome distraction.

They sat on the couch with their pizza and beer. They watched a movie and ate the pizza, not talking much. Graham was thankful for that. He wasn't ready to talk about it. And he wasn't sure what Sam knew. He knew Poppy knew about his place in time, but he and Sam had never discussed it. But he did very much enjoy Sam's company.

"Hey, I wanted to show you this. It had some of those attraction playground pieces I want to build," he said. He handed Graham his phone and showed him a video that showed another orchard that had a giant playground, a petting zoo, and other attractions. "I think we could build some of these and put them on the clearing that butts right up against the property here."

"Aye," Graham said, nodding. He handed Sam back his phone. He watched as Sam pulled up another video that gave step-by-step directions on how to build what was called a human hamster wheel. Graham was too busy thinking about the app itself to pay much attention.

"It doesn't look too hard to construct. I think we could make one of those," Sam said as he watched the video.

"Aye, we could. This app, is it all little videos?" Graham asked.

"YouTube? Yeah, you can find a video on just about anything. There are tons of videos on how to do just about anything you could think of."

"Growing up on a farm in Scotland, we didn't have the internet, so I am still learning certain things."

Sam nodded at him.

Graham took a breath and swallowed his pride. He may not have liked asking for help, but he needed to prove he belonged there. Even though Hannah did not choose him, he still needed to prove it to himself.

"I'm trying to put together some things to present Mr. Glenn with our ideas. Do you think you could maybe show me some tips?"

"Of course," Sam said.

The two of them hung out for the rest of the night. They watched a movie and finished the beer Sam had brought. Graham was glad he was there.

. . .

In the next couple of days, Graham became well acquainted with YouTube. He also became somewhat acquainted with some office software and emailing, like Sam had showed him. He managed to create a document to send that explained how he could utilize some of his land to benefit both him and the orchard. He was able to send their ideas to Mr. Glenn, and even more than that, Graham was learning the basic functions of a modern society. He may not have liked it, nor will he ever be good at it, but he knew enough to get by, and that was enough for him.

It was still cold, with snow covering the ground. Graham cared for the horses and helped Sam, but it was a slow season, and Graham, sometimes, had large amounts of time with nothing to do. So, instead of listening to Hannah read every night, he learned how to work the TV enough to get to Netflix. He came across *Outlander*. It had intrigued him when Hannah read it, so he thought it might be worth a watch. It was a bizarre experience watching the show, to say the least.

While there were some inaccuracies, it did look familiar. He had done many of the same things this band of men did. He had seen firsthand the atrocities the British doled out on those he loved. He was in this rebellion. He was glad he was brought to that time, and not Hannah to his. Watching what Jamie Frasier had to do to keep his wife safe was terrifying.

Yes, he would gladly do all the things that man had done, and quite frankly, they were more in his skill set than writing a bloody email, but here, Hannah was safe, with no threat of bodily harm, so he was thankful for that. If Hannah had been in his time, it would have been a much different story, one he didn't care to dwell on.

As he spent more time watching the show, he began to learn more about the rebellion and the Jacobites. He watched the Battle of Culloden and saw that it was the end of the highlander's way of life. He knew when he returned, the battle would be mere weeks away. He would either lose his life in battle, or he would lose his entire way of life. He wasn't sure which was worse.

He began to research the battle itself. Maybe if he knew how, he could change things, but he didn't hold out hope. He just felt adrift. He would go back and fight because it was the right thing to do, but he wanted to stay. No choice felt right without Hannah.

HE WAS COMING in from the barn one day in late February when he saw a little flashing light next to the telephone. Upon inspection, he saw a message—from who, he didn't know, but he pushed the button that said play.

"Hi, Graham, this is Josie. I didn't have your cell number, but I needed to talk to you. I'm not sure what happened between you and Hannah, but I know you are still in town for a little while. Anyway, I don't know if Hannah has told you, but our dad just had a major heart attack. He is in surgery now. I can't get there. Brett and my mom are at the hospital, but you know Hannah. I'm sure she is freaking out and trying to be Wonder Woman and take care of everyone. My mom is a mess—because, of course she is—and I'm sure Brett won't think to check in with Hannah, so I just thought you might be able to help her. It didn't seem like you guys had a major falling out, just a timing issue, so if you could check on Hannah, it would be appreciated."

The message ended. He hit the button to listen to it again and raked his hand through his hair. He felt desperate to get to Hannah. He had watched enough TV and movies to know a heart attack is bad, and surgery is worse. He fumbled with his phone and managed to call Poppy to let her know what had happened. Sam took him to the train station. He had been to the godforsaken city once before with Hannah, so he could figure it out again.

He boarded the train to the city armed with his wee pocket contraption, Hannah's apartment address and an app Sam called Uber. He was going to be there for her because Josie was right. He knew Hannah. He knew things with her father were strained, and she would be upset. She would be taking care of everyone. He needed to take care of her.

CHAPTER 25

*I*t was late. Hannah was slogging back to her apartment. She had been at the hospital since the night before. Her dad was out of surgery, but he hadn't awoken yet. The weight of the day hung heavily on her. She had made sure her mother got dinner and helped get her set up in the hospital next to her dad, with some pillows and blankets. She knew her mom wasn't going to leave his side. It was only at her mother's insistence that she had headed back to her apartment.

Things still weren't quite right with her dad. She resented him for not supporting her and sneaking behind her back to get her the job. She was trying to let it go. When her mom called her, frantic, the night before, it was because her dad was being rushed to the hospital with a heart attack. Hannah was beside herself, and she had been ever since. But her mom was right to send her home and get some sleep.

When she turned onto her block, she saw a familiar figure on the steps of her apartment. Her heart skipped a beat. When he turned and looked at her, his red hair cascaded around his shoulders, Hannah's knees almost gave out. She stopped where she stood.

"Graham . . . what are you doing here?" she said breathlessly.

He made his way over to her in three giant strides, and she fell into his arms. Something clicked into place when he held her. The weight of the day lifted, and she let go. She started crying and clinging to him.

"Hush, mo ghrádh," he said as he stroked her hair.

"How are you here?" she asked. She pulled back to look at him.

"Josie called and left a message on the . . . the message thing. She was worried ye would be taking care of everyone and not yerself. I know she was most likely right, so I came. I wanted to be here for ye."

"Thank you," was all Hannah could say. She was emotionally wrecked from the day and from finding him there, at her apartment. "Why don't we head inside? I ordered a pizza; it should be here soon."

"Aye, let's do that."

They walked over to the door. Graham picked up his bag from the stairs while Hannah unlocked the door. They climbed the steps to her third-floor walk-up. Hannah unlocked the door and Graham followed her in.

It was a small one-bedroom apartment with an entryway that led into a living room, which had a small sofa and a chair with a coffee table and a TV on the left. On the right, a small two-person table and chairs and the tiniest kitchen Graham had ever seen. It only had room for one person to stand comfortably. Hannah put her purse down on the entry table, along with her keys, and kicked off her shoes. Graham slipped his shoes off as well and put his bag down next to them.

"Well, this is it," she said. "This is my home in the city."

Graham looked around and nodded.

"It's tiny, but it's just me, so it's fine. I think I am going to take a shower before the pizza gets here."

"All right, I will be right here."

She looked at him and squeezed his hand. She needed to reassure herself he was actually with her.

Once Hannah was out of the shower and in more comfortable clothes, she joined Graham. She was glad he was there. Of course, she was still worried about her dad, but having Graham there helped. Her phone buzzed, letting her know the pizza arrived. She went downstairs to get it.

When she came back up, Graham already had plates and water out for them, along with a bottle of wine.

"I wasn't sure what you would want to drink," he said.

"Why don't you pop that baby open?" she said as she set the pizza down in front of them.

Graham opened the bottle of wine, and Hannah found a sappy rom com to watch. She knew it would help her to take her mind off things. They ate and watched *When Harry Met Sally*, a classic.

At some point during the movie, after the pizza was long gone, Hannah must have fallen asleep. She woke up around 2 a.m., lying on Graham's chest. He had thrown a blanket over them. He was reclined, with his feet kicked up on the chair, and his head resting on a pillow against the wall. He had one arm around her, his other hand on top of hers that rested on his chest. She listened to his rhythmic breathing and the beat of his heart, then relaxed into him and drifted back to sleep.

Later that morning, she woke up, the sun streaming into her window. She looked up at Graham. He was awake this time, smiling down at her.

"I'm sorry. It seems like I fell asleep on you." Hannah bit her lip and looked at him, hoping this wouldn't be awkward.

"Aye, that ye did," he said as he absentmindedly stroked her arm. "Don't worry, I dinna mind."

Hannah sat up and stretched. She had a kink in her neck from sleeping like that, but she had a feeling that, if Graham had not been there, she would have tossed and turned all night.

"What is yer plan for the day?" Graham asked.

"Well," she said as she checked her phone. "My mom said she would text when my dad was awake, and nothing yet. I think I might try and catch up on a few work emails and head back to the hospital."

"All right, you get some work done, and I will make ye some breakfast," Graham said with a small squeeze to her arm.

"You don't have to do that, Graham, I can just eat some Pop-Tarts and coffee. It's fine."

"I know I dinna have to, but I thought ye need to fill yer belly with something other than whatever Pop-Tarts are. I will make ye some coffee, though. How about some eggs and whatever else I can find in that wee closet of a kitchen while ye do some work?"

"Thanks, Graham. That sounds amazing."

Graham stood and folded the blanket. He set it on the chair and started for the kitchen. Hannah reached out and took his hand.

"No, really, thank you, Graham. Thank you for coming all this way. I still don't know how you got here by yourself. I know you hate the city."

"Aye, I do. That has not changed, but Sam took me to the train station and showed me how to use my wee pocket contraption to call an Uber? I think it was. Anyway, nothing would stop me from being here and helping ye when I am still able to," he said to her with a wink.

Hannah fought the urge to kiss him. She shook the

thought and got out her laptop. After walking over to her dining room table, she plugged it in and got to work answering emails. There was an important meeting she was missing. They were understanding, but she wanted to make sure everyone was briefed and had her files beforehand. They probably did, but at least that way, she felt like she was doing something.

"Ye don't have much food here, Hannah. What do ye eat?" Graham asked with an amused smile on his face.

"Shut up! I don't really have time to cook much. I eat a lot of takeout."

"I can see that." Graham said, sniffing a takeout container, scrunching his face.

"Stop it. I'm a busy woman."

"Correct me if I'm wrong, but busy people do still require food."

"Don't bother me. I have work to do," she said, giving him a silly grin, pointing to her laptop.

"Aye, ye do yer work, and I will make ye food," he said. He kissed the top of her head. Hannah just about jumped out of her skin at this small gesture. "I'm sorry, Hannah, I should not have kissed ye." The smile fell from his face, and he turned back to the kitchen.

"It's okay, old habits and all," she said quietly.

About ten minutes later, Graham brought over two plates with eggs, toast, and a cup of coffee and sat down opposite her. Hannah closed her laptop and slipped it back into her bag.

"So, how can I help?" Graham asked.

"Well, I am going to head back to the hospital." As if on cue, her phone buzzed with a text from her mother letting her know her father was awake.

"Looks like my dad is up, so I am going to go."

She stopped and looked at Graham. Just the sight of him

filled her heart and split it into two at the same time. She felt selfish, but she wanted him by her side. His presence just had a way of grounding her.

"Will you come with me?" she asked tentatively.

"Of course, if ye want me there, that's where I will be. Although, I will say, I have seen yer modern hospitals in some of the shows on the TV, and it makes it look akin to a torture chamber."

"Yeah . . . that's fair. It also means a subway ride."

Graham groaned. "Only for you, Hannah Glenn." He solemnly shook his head.

"I really do appreciate it, Graham."

"Dinna mention it."

Hannah was much more relaxed, knowing her dad was recovering, having a good night's sleep, and having Graham there. Things just felt lighter with him as he helped her to shoulder the burden.

He seemed much better on the subway this time. Last time, before the wedding, he seemed a little cranky and skittish. He still seemed generally irritated by the whole thing but much better. She was curious to see how he would do in the hospital.

They made their way into the massive hospital, and she took Graham's hand. Maybe she shouldn't have, but she thought they both might have needed an anchor right then. They made their way to the elevator.

"How ya holding up, big guy?" She gave him a gentle nudge.

He looked down at her and raised an eyebrow. She smiled at him and chuckled.

They made their way to her father's hospital room. Hannah could hear her mom on the phone. It sounded like she was talking to her brother.

"Yeah, he's doing better. He's been up for a while. He's reading the paper right now. Hannah should be here soon."

Hannah knocked as they walked fully into the room.

"Oh, here she is now." Her mom let out a squeak. "Oh, and it looks like Graham is here with her. I'll call you back later. Bye, sweetheart."

"Hi," Hannah whispered as she walked in.

"Hi, Hannah. Graham, I'm surprised to see you here."

"Aye, Josie called me to tell me about what had happened to Mr. Glenn, and I thought you and Hannah might like some help."

"Did she really? That's surprisingly thoughtful of her," her mother said.

Hannah chuckled.

"That's what I thought, too." She made her way over to the bed to see her dad. "Hi, Dad, how are you feeling?"

"Like shit."

"Well, ya look like shit, too," Hannah said back with a soft smile.

"Don't worry. Doc said I'll be good as new. Didn't they, honey?"

"They did, but not quite new." She gave Richard a sweet, knowing smile. "They said he came through the surgery well. He's in for a couple days for observation and then home and no more cigars." She said that last part pointedly at him.

They visited while the never-ending parade of specialists and nurses and the poking and prodding continued. Hannah looked over at Graham, who had a faraway look in his eyes.

"Hey, Mom, have you eaten anything today?"

"I haven't yet. I just don't want to miss any of the doctors or nurses," she said.

"Okay, Graham and I will walk to the cafeteria and get you some food."

"Oh, that would be lovely. Thank you, Hannah. Thank you both for being here. I know I can always count on you."

"No problem, Mom." She looked at her dad, who had drifted off. "We will be right back with some food."

"Oh, no rush. Take your time."

As they made their way back to the elevator, Graham bent down to Hannah's ear. "I see I was right. It is akin to a torture chamber."

Hannah chuckled and lightly elbowed Graham. He put his hand on the small of her back and guided her into the elevator.

They brought her food and spent a few hours visiting with her parents. Hannah couldn't help but chuckle every time a nurse came in for vitals, and her mother would share their whole life's story. Brett dropped off an overnight bag for his mom with a change of clothes and toiletries on his lunch break. Josie called and Facetimed. It was getting close to dinner.

"Why don't you guys head home? I don't think much else is going on here for the night."

"Do you want to go get food, Mom? You haven't been out of this room. It might be good for you to get out and move around a bit," said Hannah.

"I don't want to leave your father."

"Go ahead, Joanne. Graham, would you mind taking her to the cafeteria?" Richard asked.

"Of course," Graham said with a warm smile.

"Banana can stay here and keep her old dad company."

Graham and Joanne left as the door clicked behind them. She went and took the seat next to her dad. The Rangers game was on TV, and she could hear the sportscasters coming from the speaker near the bed.

"The Rangers, huh? I haven't seen you watch hockey for a while."

"Yeah, there are lots of things I haven't done for a while that I think I might start doing."

"Oh, yeah," she said.

"Yes. And, Hannah, I owe you an apology."

Hannah looked at him, eyes wide. She was a bit taken aback.

"No, you don't, Dad."

"Yes," he said, taking her hand. "I do . . . you know I love you, but I think I may have been too hard on you."

"Dad, please don't. It's fine. I know you love me, and you were right. I am enjoying my job at the new firm. We're all good." His hand felt weak in hers, which was still hooked up to so many things.

"No, Hannah, let me get this out. You told me you didn't want to be a lawyer anymore because it didn't make you happy, and I didn't listen. All I have ever wanted is for you, my children, to be happy. I see Brett. He has a good job, he works too hard, but I know he is happy running the business he built. I look at your sister. She's a bit of a fart in a whirlwind, but she is happy. I don't want to change her; I just hope she finds her passion someday. But I think I looked at you differently. I have always seen so much of myself in you. I see someone who gets the job done. I see someone who puts in the work," he said, squeezing her hand.

"I see someone who cares. I liked that you refused my help, no matter how many times I offered it. I took pride in your work ethic, but I think I forgot to check in to see if doing that made you happy." He stopped talking, and Hannah could see he was getting a little choked up.

"Dad, it's fine. I'm happy," she said, knowing it wasn't the full truth.

"Are you? Because you told me you weren't, and I didn't listen. I pushed you and sprung this job on you because I thought it was what you wanted. I thought I knew what was best for you, but I didn't stop to think that YOU know what's best for you. You always have. Hannah if you don't want to be a lawyer, please don't be a lawyer. If you want to keep the job with Lucy Chen, then please keep the job but not because you are trying to make me happy. It needs to be what makes you happy."

A tear rolled down, tickling her cheek. Richard picked up his hand to wipe it away.

"Thank you, Dad."

"I just want you to stop and think about it. You don't have to make any decisions right now. Also, I want to give you something."

"Dad, please, I'm fine. I am making good money now."

Her dad took her hand again until Hannah was looking at him. He made sure she was listening.

"Hannah, stop. I gave your brother start-up money. I give your sister money all the time. You have never asked for anything, and I know you won't. But I have decided, I am going to give you the farmhouse and all the land that goes with it."

"What?"

"You have always loved that place, Hannah. I was always going to leave it to you anyway, but let's just say it's yours sooner. As soon as I'm out of here, I am going to start the paperwork for it to officially be yours. So, if you want to be a writer and live out there, it's yours to do so. Now I do hope that you will let us come visit for the holidays and maybe even game day," he said with a wink. "But it is yours"

"I don't know what to say, Dad."

"Say thank you and say that you will find what makes you happy. I very recently learned that life is too short to spend time on things that don't make you happy. And you, Banana, deserve all the happiness in the world."

"Thank you, Daddy," she said, hugging him.

"And, Hannah, one last thing. I don't know exactly what is going on with you and Graham, but I think he is good for you. I see the way you guys look out for each other. Finding someone who has your back and loves you, flaws and all, isn't easy."

"Please, Dad, I can't talk about Graham," she said, barely holding it together.

"Okay, I said what I needed to say." He patted her on the hand. "Now, let's get back to the game. It's been a long time since we watched a game together."

They settled into a comfortable silence. Hannah was relieved to have mended things with her dad. The conversation was going to have her thinking for quite some time.

HANNAH WAS quiet the rest of the night. Her mind was hard at work, mulling over what her dad said. She was so sure she knew what she needed to do, but everything seemed to be falling apart.

Graham was leaving. What good was the house in the country if it didn't mean being with him? She could easily go on working this job, but living a tolerable life on autopilot isn't really living. Just three months with Graham had shown her what it felt like to come alive. She didn't realize she had been living a half-life, but if that is what living could feel like, she hadn't felt that in her entire life.

Graham was in her tiny kitchen, putting away dinner dishes. They grabbed Chinese takeout on their way home, and introducing it was definitely a good time. She smiled just thinking about watching him try an egg roll and the other food they ordered. She was finishing up some work, and she just couldn't stop thinking. She couldn't decide what she wanted and how to get out of her own head. Her head wasn't in a great place right then.

Finishing up, she found Graham leaning against the kitchen door frame looking at her. He looked incredible. What she wouldn't give for one last time with him. He had the power to turn her brain off. Maybe he could fuck some clarity into her . . . that was a bad idea . . . was it, though? Yes! Bad idea!

"How are ye doing, mo ghrádh?"

And with that, she lost all resolve. That's all it took: one look, one utterance of endearment, and she was gone.

"I just can't shut my brain off," she said, still trying to figure out her decision.

"Well, why don't ye start by turning that thing off," he said, gesturing to her laptop. "We can watch a movie or maybe ye can read to me. I see a shelf full of the romance novels ye read to me at the farm."

Okay . . . she was going for it.

"Or . . . we could do something else we used to do at the farm?"

He looked at her, and his eyes flashed with hunger for a moment but then returned.

"Are ye certain? It might not be a good idea."

"You're right, it might be a really bad idea," she said as she got up before stepping over to him and putting her hands on his chest. "But it could turn my brain off . . . and, Graham, I really need to turn my brain off."

She fisted his shirt and pulled him to her. She lifted her face to his and kissed him gently at first but then she opened her mouth and licked his bottom lip. He moved his hands down to her waist and pulled her into him. He opened his mouth, and when their tongues met, Hannah moaned. He stopped and pulled away. Hannah ached at his absence. She needed it. She needed him.

"What is it ye are asking, Hannah? I need ye to say it."

"I need you to help me stop thinking. I need you to fuck me, Graham."

Graham growled, took her mouth, and kissed her hungrily. Hannah could feel the spark dancing between them. Whatever was between them was something she had never experienced before, and she knew she never would again. She would take him to her bed one last time before he was gone forever. It might have been a bad idea, and it might have made things harder, but all that mattered right then was in that room between them. She pulled her mouth from his, and he kissed her neck, then bit her at the sensitive place at the base of her neck. Hannah had an empty throbbing feeling inside her, and she needed him. Now. God, she had missed this.

"And, Graham, don't be gentle."

Graham needed no further instruction. He picked her up, and she wrapped her legs around him. Hannah was not small. She had never been with someone who even attempted to pick her up or was even remotely capable of picking her up, but she knew Graham had her. He fumbled his way into the bedroom, their mouths connecting. They bumped into the door frame, knocking some things off her dresser, but she didn't even look to see. He set her down on the bed.

"Take off your clothes," he rasped, loosening his belt.

Hannah took off her shirt and unbuttoned her pants. She stood to pull them down, but Graham, who was in only boxer shorts—very tented boxer shorts, at that—yanked her pants down in one swift motion and kneeled between her legs. He pushed her back onto the bed, took one of her legs, and put it over his shoulder. The other one, he pushed far to the side.

He looked at her. "Christ, Hannah, you have the most perfect cunt."

He ran one finger down her seam, then pushed in and felt the slick heat, and they both moaned. He circled her clit with his finger, then it slipped lower and slipped inside of her. *Oh my god, it feels so good.* Then he added another finger and explored her, finding her G-spot. Then she felt his tongue lick her and circle her clit. She cried out. It wasn't going to take her long to come. He gently sucked her clit into his mouth, swirling his tongue, his finger working her inside. She felt the tingling building inside of her. One last suck of her clit, and she was driven over the edge. She cried out as he chased her pleasure.

The world had long since fallen away. All that existed all that had ever existed was right there in that room. The way he touched her and the way he made her feel were things of storybook love. As the final wave crashed over her, Graham pulled out his fingers and stood before her.

"Are ye finished, Hannah, or do ye want more?"

There were no words left to think.

"More."

"Good. Move up the bed." He motioned his head as Hannah scooted up her bed.

He kissed his way up her body. Stopping to pay proper attention to her breasts, he rubbed one nipple between his fingers and sucked the other into his mouth. The electricity swelled in her again. She could feel him at her entrance. He moved just a little, and it brushed against her clit. Hannah gasped and dug her nails into his back.

"Is this what you want?"

"Mmm-hmm."

He positioned himself at her entrance and pushed in. Slowly, at first, until he was sheathed fully in her. She cried out. She was filled with such want and need for this man. He pulled out and slammed back into her. She had told him not to be gentle, and he was not going to be. She cried with pleasure. She could feel nothing but him. He filled every single one of her senses. She bit his shoulder hard, and he slammed into her again.

"Don't stop."

And he didn't. He kept thrusting into her, picking up speed, fucking her harder than she had ever been fucked and would be ruined for the rest of her life because no one would ever make her feel this way again. None of that mattered, not with this man inside of her wrecking her and building her back up. She could hear nothing but his heavy breathing and their flesh smacking together. His finger dug into her soft hips; she was sure there would be a mark, but she wanted marks. She wanted to be marked by this man, to be claimed by him.

"Harder."

He growled and pushed in even harder. She didn't know it could feel like that. She thought he might fuck her right in half, but she didn't care. She bit him again. Her nails dug into his back, her body on the cusp of an explosion. One last hard thrust sent her over the edge, and she cried out. He kept going for two more thrusts, then he cried out as he went rigid and came inside of her. She could feel his cock pulsing, and all was right with the world. This man had just fucked every single thought from her head.

He collapsed onto her shoulder; his breathing labored. Then he raised his head and gave her a kiss. The sweetest, most loving kiss she had ever been given. Then he pulled out, fell to her side, and gathered her into his arms. She felt so safe and cared for. Her brain had definitely turned off for the night.

IN THE COLD light of day, things looked a little different. She lay there, looking at him. He was still asleep. How could he leave? Hannah knew he didn't belong, but she had never given him the option. Yes, he was talking about wanting to get back to his own time, but he had to know that whatever was between them was a once-in-a-lifetime feeling . . . Hell, it was a once-in-the-universe feeling. Maybe that old witch knew what she was doing.

Hannah was going to try. She had a lot to figure out, but she was going to figure it out. Sam's wedding was in three weeks. She had three weeks to make him want to stay, but first, she needed to deal with things in the city. He had planned on going back to the farm that day. She was going to find a way to fix this. They belonged together. She wasn't sure about much, but she was sure of that.

CHAPTER 26

*G*raham was on the train home. The raindrops raced down the window as Graham reflected on his time in the city. He was relieved to get out of the city, but he had been thinking since the night before. He didn't want to leave Hannah. He never had. It seemed like it was what she wanted, but they never had a real conversation about it. It was time that happened.

When she came back for the wedding, he was going to leave it all on the table. If staying there meant he had to live in the overcrowded, godforsaken city, he would do it. He had to help her to see that whatever it was between them was too important to cast aside. He just had to figure out how he was going to do that.

Back at the farm, he helped Sam with some of the last touches for the wedding. They were getting married outside and having the reception in one of the warehouses before it filled up with this year's crop. Graham helped clean it out and build some platforms for the ceremony and the reception. The two men were busy hanging lights.

"You are really leaving after the wedding?" Sam asked as he climbed down the ladder.

"Actually . . . I'm hoping plans might change."

"Oh, yeah? It would be great keeping you around," he said, tossing him a water bottle.

"Aye, I have decided to talk to Hannah after yer wedding. I intend to see if she would be interested in giving things a real go and me staying here. Hopefully that doesn't mean in that city, but I would be there for her."

"I hope it doesn't mean in the city, either, man. You are a pretty useful neighbor," he said, handing Graham another strand of lights.

"I sent Mr. Glenn the proposal that we talked about."

"That's good. I think we could really make the orchard an attraction and not just a place to get apples and other produce."

"Aye, I would like that, but first, I need Hannah to say she wants me to stay." Graham tried to push away the pit in his stomach that formed every time he thought about it.

"Don't worry, man, I have known Hannah her whole life. Her and my sister have spent every summer damn near inseparable. I have met some of Hannah's other boyfriends, and they were all idiots. None of them ever deserved her. You guys are different. She's different with you. You will work it out."

Graham nodded and started back up the ladder to hang the lights. He hoped Sam was right and that Hannah's feelings were as strong as his. He had to show her he was capable of fitting into this time and being a good man for her.

They finished up preparation for the wedding. Hannah was getting in town Friday afternoon for the rehearsal dinner. Graham wished more than ever that he could drive because he desperately wanted to be the one to pick up Hannah. He felt nervous about what was to come. He had charged into battle with the Red Coats and had never felt the nerves he felt right then. If the six long weeks they spent apart were any indication of what life will be like without her, he did not intend to do that again. He had to convince her he belonged. That he could take care of her and provide a life for them.

He saw Poppy's car pull up and went out to get her bags. Poppy popped the trunk when she saw him coming, but she and Hannah were talking. Poppy looked back at him and winked. *What was that all about?* he thought to himself.

Hannah came right into Graham's arms. His heart jolted at the ease of their reunion. He unloaded two large suitcases and a hanging bag. It did not appear to be a weekend bag, but he would try not to read into that. He needed to woo Hannah. He needed to show he could fit into her life here, and thus, the countdown started.

That night was the rehearsal dinner, and the next day was the wedding, with the following day being the equinox. He had till then to convince her they should be together.

"How was the train?" he asked.

"Oh, it was good. I took some time to read a book and relax."

"That's good. Ye need to relax more."

Hannah opened the door for him, and he took her bags upstairs.

Hannah had been upstairs getting ready since she got home. Graham was all ready to go. He was wearing the suit he wore to the first wedding they had attended together. Hannah came down the stairs in the green dress she wore to the same wedding. It hugged Hannah in all the right places, emphasizing her curves. Graham had thought the dress was indecent the first time he saw it, but this time he just wanted to take her upstairs and rip it off her. But that was not wooing, and that was his goal for the next two days.

"You, mo ghrádh, take my breath away. You are the bonniest lass I have ever seen." He reached for her hand and pressed a kiss to the back of it. He saw the flush of Hannah's cheek. He knew how she felt. This fire that existed between them was powerful.

"I remember the first time I saw ye in that dress. It was the first night I kissed ye," he said in a low rumble.

"Hmm, it was," Hannah hummed with a glint in her eye. "It was also the night you punched Roger Glass's son-in-law, and I'm not sure I ever thanked you for the brutish act of Scottish chivalry."

"Well, ye may have called it brutish, but ye definitely left out the chivalry part."

"Well, thank you, Graham, for defending my honor," she said in a sultry tone that shot straight to Graham's cock.

She leaned into him and gave him a deep kiss, pressing her body into his. Graham felt her breast press up against his chest, and her soft belly pressed into his growing erection. He would not rip her dress off and take her on the table. No. He wouldn't. That was not wooing, but as she opened her mouth and licked into his, he broke away from her.

"Much more of this, and we will never make it to dinner," he said, using every last bit of willpower to stop kissing her.

"You're right, maybe later." Hannah grabbed his tie and pulled him down for one last kiss.

Graham pulled his head back and handed Hannah her clutch.

"It's a wee bit cold out there tonight," Graham said as he held Hannah's wrap for her.

She looked at him with interest and slipped it over her shoulders.

They headed out the door for the rehearsal dinner.

After a night of pleasant conversations and heartfelt toasts, it was time to head home. Graham and Hannah walked hand in hand to the car.

"You and Sam have certainly gotten to be good friends since you've been here."

"Aye, we have. He's easy to get along with"

"Yeah, probably because he doesn't talk much."

Graham looked at her. He found Sam easy to talk to and thought he had plenty of things to say.

"He says enough."

"Ahhh, I get it. Men of few words actually talk when they are together."

"I have been accused of many things in my life. Being a man of few words has never been one of them, mo ghrádh."

"No, you're right. You talk plenty. I remember how much I just wanted you to keep your mouth closed when you first came."

"Aye, well someone had to tell ye how a proper woman should behave." He grinned at her. This also may have not been part of the wooing, but he could not pass up a chance to get a rise out of Hannah. He loved it when she got fiery.

"Excuse me! We have been over this." She stood with her hands on her hips.

He laughed. "Yer awfully bonny when yer all fired up, but it's all right. Ye've shown me the error of my brutish ways." He took her hand and kissed it again.

They pulled up to the farm. He got out and opened Hannah's door and helped her out of the car.

"Well, aren't you chivalrous tonight."

"I'm just treating ye as ye deserve to be treated, mo ghrádh. You deserve all this and more."

Hannah seemed a bit taken aback by that. Was he coming on too strong? He just needed her to see that he could take care of her. That he had things he could offer in this time before it was too late.

Once they got in the house, Hannah turned on him with a look so hot he almost burst into flames. She walked over to him, walked him back against the door, and kissed him. She pressed her body into his, fisted her hands in his hair, pulled her face to her, and took his mouth. He was so taken aback. He pushed her hips away from him, cock already hard in his pants.

"What has gotten into ye, woman?"

"Graham, I just want to be with you. I want to feel you. Right now. I want you inside of me. Right now."

That was definitely not part of the wooing Graham had in mind, but he wasn't going to pass it up. He grabbed her body, pulled her into him, and kissed her. She pushed him up against the door, pressing her lush, soft body into him, and he relished her warmth.

Then she moved her hands down to his waist band and undid his pants. She reached in, took out his cock, and stroked it hard. Graham groaned and pushed into her hand. She stopped kissing him, looked at him, and bit her lip. Then she dropped down to her knees.

It definitely wasn't wooing her, but there was no way he was stopping it. He gathered up Hannah's long blonde hair into his fist. He looked down and saw her looking back up at him, her eyes scorching him. It was undeniably hot. What had gotten into her? She took all of him that she could into her mouth, and Graham moaned. Then she started working him with her hand, licking and sucking on the tip. He was going to come in her mouth, and he needed to make her come first.

"Hannah," he groaned.

She stopped and looked up at him. He brought her up to him, claimed her mouth, then walked her back. He lifted her dress up and scooted her back onto the counter. He could feel how wet she was through her panties. He hooked his thumbs on the side of the lace panties and ripped them off. Then he lined himself up to her core and pushed in.

"Fuck, Graham," she cried out.

He was not going to last much longer. He took his finger and worked slow circles over her clit, working his cock in and out.

She threw her head back. "Oh my god, Graham."

Hearing his name on her lips like that felt right. They belonged together. He felt the tightening at the base of his cock, and he knew he would not be able to last much longer. Then she cried out, and her pussy pulsed around him. He followed her right over the edge.

Breathless, he slumped onto her shoulder and kissed it.

"Hannah Glenn, what has gotten into ye?"

He got off her and put a tender kiss on her mouth. It was only then, as Hannah hopped off the counter and adjusted her dress, he realized they were both fully dressed, with the exception of Hannah's underwear that lay torn and discarded on the floor.

CHAPTER 27

Operation Make Graham Stay was a go. He was trying to be a gentleman, but Hannah had been able to tempt him. Once on the kitchen counter, one more time in bed, and one more time that morning, when she had surprised him in the shower.

Hannah never really got the appeal of shower sex. Someone was always cold, and with being a bigger person, the logistics were always off. But that morning, when Graham was in the shower, she just stepped in, and he was dumbfounded. Hannah loved the look of shock and lust on his face. She kissed him, then dropped to her knees and sucked him off until he came all over her tits. She then stood, washed off, and got out before he even knew what hit him. Hannah had never thrown herself at a guy so shamelessly in her life, and she was enjoying herself.

Hannah was downstairs in the kitchen, making breakfast, when Graham came down the stairs in jeans, boots, and a Smith's Orchard hoody, his wet hair pulled up in a top not on his head.

"Can ye make mine to go? I told Sam I would meet him at nine to set up for the ceremony."

Hannah popped an English muffin in the toaster to make him a breakfast sandwich. She turned around and gave him a smoldering look.

"Oh, no ye don't," Graham said as he put his hand up and backed away. "I have places to be this morning. I know that look. And ye drained me in the shower . . . and in your bed . . . and, well, on this very counter."

Hannah smiled at him and turned around to flip the bacon.

"I didn't hear you complaining," she said over her shoulder.

"Aye, and ye never will hear me complain about such a thing," he said, slipping in behind her and snaking his arms around her waist.

She relaxed into his embrace. He had to feel this. He had to feel how they belonged together. One more day to convince him. That night, after the wedding, she would ask him to stay.

"Good," she said.

Then she turned around and put a piece of bacon in his mouth. Sex and bacon . . . what better tools are there to convince a man not to leave you and time travel back to the 1700s?

He ate the bacon as Hannah assembled his breakfast sandwich. Graham got a to-go cup from the cupboard and poured himself some coffee.

"I should be back soon. We are just putting out chairs and setting up."

"Okay, Poppy is coming over. We are going to get ready together."

"All right, lass. I will see ye when I return," he said before giving her a tender kiss on top of her head.

About thirty minutes later, the door opened. Poppy walked in, carrying a big makeup bag. She had on some leggings and a button-down shirt. Her hair was freshly braided, with flowers tucked in. They headed up to Hannah's room to finish getting ready.

Hannah was curling her own hair while Poppy sat on her bed, scrolling her phone.

"I had to come over early before Jackson made me move one more thing. I mean, don't get me wrong I love him, but he's being a little much right now. Sam and Graham are over there moving everything. They have moved the ceremony chairs twice now."

Hannah only half listened. Her mind was definitely on something else—someone else, to be precise. Doubt crept in. When she was with Graham and could see how he looked at her, she felt sure he would stay, but when he was gone, it seemed like a big ask, like maybe she wasn't worth staying there for. He had a family, a whole entire life, and here, he only had her. Plus, there was the problem of him not existing in this time. There would be no record of him here or in Scotland. Graham MacNeil did not exist in this time —no birth certificate, nothing. That further complicated an already complicated situation. But she knew that, when she was with him, they belonged together and that they could figure the rest out.

"Earth to Hannah," Poppy said.

"I'm sorry, I was just thinking about something," she said.

"Clearly, what's going on? Is it Graham? I mean, of course it's Graham. He leaves soon, right?"

"Tomorrow."

"Damn, I didn't realize it was so soon. How are you holding up?"

"Well . . . I am going to ask him to stay. Tonight, after the wedding."

"I knew he wasn't going anywhere. You guys are so great together. I need to go to the ren faire next year and get my own spell from that witch."

"Maybe be a little more specific than I was."

"Nah, you got a fairytale, Hannah."

"I did . . . but only if he stays, and that's a big if."

"It's not. Anyone can see the way he looks at you. I mean, I thought you guys were going to have sex in the car as soon as you left the rehearsal dinner."

"Well . . . we made it in the door, at least," Hannah said with a smirk on her face.

"Man . . . I need to get laid," Poppy groaned.

"I saw you and Josh is he still engaged? It didn't seem so when I saw you two at karaoke. Is he going to be there tonight?"

"He's not engaged, but Hannah . . . he's your ex-boyfriend. I can't do that."

"Poppy, we had a summer fling years ago. I have no claim, and if things don't work out with Graham, I will have to become a nun because I'll be ruined forever."

"Are you sure?" she asked.

"Totally ruined . . . but also, yes, I am sure. Josh a great guy."

Poppy got oddly quiet and went back to doing her makeup, and Hannah finished curling her hair.

POPPY HAD ALREADY LEFT. It was just about time for the wedding, and Hannah was finishing up her makeup and getting dressed. She had heard Graham come home and hop in the shower. He then got ready in the next room.

She was going for it in that dress. It was more cleavage than she had usually shown. It was a royal-blue wrap dress, and she was wearing the necklace Graham had given her. It rested right above her cleavage. She looked in the mirror, and she looked hot. There was no way he was going to be able to keep his hands off her. She examined herself, took a deep breath, and turned to head downstairs.

When she got to the top of the stairs, she looked down and saw Graham looking up to her. *Holy shit.* She thought she was going to take his breath away, but there he stood, his red hair pulled back, wearing a modern kilt with the dress shirt and suit jacket. He looked amazing. He looked like her highlander but also like he belonged there with her.

She stepped down the stairs but missed her footing. Her foot slipped out from beneath her. She skidded down a couple of steps until her ass hit the stairs and quickly slid down the rest.

"Are ye all right?" Graham said, helping her to her feet, examining her for pain.

"Yeah, I'm fine," she said, rubbing her butt. "I think my pride hurts more than anything."

"Well, in that case." He took her hand and kissed it. "You look absolutely stunning."

"You look pretty incredible yourself. Is that the same kilt?"

"Aye, Jackson got it cleaned and then helped me find the modern touches, but I still have some of my old pieces with it," he said. He adjusted his sporran and straightened his cufflinks. He smoothed his hair.

"It's perfect, just like you, old world and new world rolled into one."

He kissed her, that familiar spark dancing between them.

"Shall we?" he said as he put his arm out for Hannah.

She smiled and threaded her arm through his. Hannah hoped he would want to stay. They belonged together. She had one more night to convince him.

The ceremony was beautiful—cold but beautiful. People

had finished eating and danced. Sam and Jackson danced, and Hannah tried not to cry. She had cried for most of the ceremony. She had never cried at weddings before. She blamed Graham for this.

As the song ended, the DJ came on the microphone and said, "Next up we have a special request. I am told to say, 'Hannah, you have to,' from Poppy and Jackson."

Graham and Hannah turned their heads to the dance floor. Poppy was already making her way to the floor.

"No! A karaoke bar is one thing. I am not doing the routine at the wedding."

"Come on, Hannah, do this, and we will leave you alone for the Macarena and the Cupid Shuffle."

"Well, I like to do the Cupid Shuffle," Hannah protested.

By then, the crowd had joined in, cheering Hannah on.

"I dinna think ye are getting out of this one, lass," Graham said with a gentle laugh and an encouraging hand on her back.

"Fine!"

Poppy was already over at the table, pulling Hannah onto the dance floor. After the first verse, thankfully, some of Jackson's nieces joined them on the dance floor, and before long, the dance floor was full. Hannah saw Graham leaning against a pole next to the dance floor looking at her. She made her way over to him and pulled him onto the dance floor. He looked uncomfortable. Fast dancing was not something he enjoyed, but he tried for her. She was going to shake it for him, though. Operation Make Graham Stay was still in full force.

As the night went on, they enjoyed each other. They ate cake and watched people dance. Hannah noticed that Josh was paying attention to Poppy, and that made her smile. Poppy deserved a guy like Josh.

A slow song came on, and Graham took Hannah's hand

and led her out onto the dance floor. He was dancing like a gentleman, holding her close but not too close, keeping his hands in the safe zone. Hannah decided to turn it up a notch.

She slid her hand into his hair and whispered, "Does what you're wearing under your kilt match what I'm wearing under my dress? Because, if the answer is nothing, then it does." Then she licked and nipped his earlobe. Hannah smiled as he groaned.

"Hannah Glenn, it is one thing to hide my feelings for ye in pants, but there will be no makin' me decent in this kilt if ye keep it up."

She bit her lip and smiled.

"What has gotten into ye? You wanton woman."

Hannah raised her eyebrows and Graham groaned and put a little distance between them.

They stayed longer and had a few drinks. Hannah could feel the nerves setting in. If she stayed, she would drink more, and that would not help things. Most of the people left were family. Graham said goodbye to Sam, giving him a hug. It made Hannah smile. She was just thinking about the brutish highlander, who had woken up in her barn six months before, who was there, hugging Sam, his gay best friend, after helping him set up his wedding.

"You guys headed out?" Poppy asked.

Hannah turned around.

"Yeah, I think we are gonna go. I see Josh is still around."

"I'm sure it's nothing."

"Right," Hannah said with a smile.

"So, are you gonna ask Graham to stay? How are you feeling?"

"Yeah, I have to." Her voice caught, and her sinuses burned. "I just love him." She tried to blink away tears and doubt. Poppy wrapped her arms around her.

"You got this. He loves you, and you will get your happy

ending if you are brave enough to take it."

"Thank you," she said.

She took a deep breath, then felt Graham's large hand on the small of her back.

"Are ye ready, mo ghrádh?"

"Yeah." She pulled Poppy into one last hug for some self-confidence.

"I'll call you tomorrow," she said.

"All right. I'll talk to you later. Bye, Graham," Poppy said.

And, in true Graham fashion, he smiled at her and bowed. On the car ride home, Hannah couldn't bring herself to try to seduce Graham. She was too nervous about what he was going to say. This could be their last night together, and that was not a thought that she entertain. He had to stay. She would find a way to be okay if he wanted to go back, but she would be much better if he stayed.

She pulled up to the house and put the car in park. She sat there for a moment, trying to get herself under control. Graham opened the door to help her out. She took his hand. She could do this. *Graham, stay with me. Graham, don't ever leave. Graham, let's live here and have lots of babies and goats and stuff.* She wasn't quite sure where that last one came from. She was losing her mind.

He held her hand and walked her up to the front door. He stopped and looked down at her. If Hannah hadn't been so caught up in her own nerves, she would have seen the same nervousness in his eyes. He gave her a gentle, loving kiss, the same kiss that they had right in front of this door after their first official date.

As they walked in, Hannah saw a binder sitting on the table. Her name was featured prominently on the cover.

"What is this?"

"Hannah, I have something I would like to talk to you about."

CHAPTER 28

"*G*raham, what is this?"

He looked at her for the first time. Her eyes looked unsure. She hadn't yet picked up the binder. That wasn't a good sign, but he had to do this.

"Hannah, I have to tell you something."

She just looked at him and nodded.

"Read it."

She picked up the binder and opened to the first page. Graham knew she was reading his top ten reasons for wanting to stay here.

10 Reasons I Should Stay with You

One - The first reason is the most important reason. I love you, Hannah Glenn.

Two - I'm useful. I take good care of the horses and the stable.

Three - I take good care of you, Hannah, in a number of ways.

Four - Speaking of those ways. The sex. Hannah, that alone could be all the reasons.

Five - I mastered this modern kitchen and will bring you coffee in bed every morning.

Six - I learned how to ride the train to come visit you in the city. (Unless you would like me to move there with you, which I would do so that has to say something about my intentions.)

Seven - I learned how to use my wee pocket contraption, so I will be available to you whenever you need me. I have been learning modern technology and will continue to make an effort to be a modern man . . . mostly.

Eight - I will always support you. I believe in your dreams, Hannah, I just want to be here to be your partner.

Nine - You clearly need me for the chopping of the wood . . . which I will do frequently . . . with my shirt off. I know how much you like that.

Ten - Hannah, my tenth reason is the same as the first. I love you.

I TRULY BELIEVE we are meant to be together. I was brought here for a reason. I was brought here to be your partner, here in this time. The feeling between us is rare, indeed. The magic that dances between us when we are together is the magic of two souls destined to be. I believe that with my whole heart, Hannah Glenn, we are meant to be.

HANNAH LOOKED UP AT HIM, her eyes full of tears and confusion.

"Hannah Glenn, I think I have loved ye from the moment I saw ye. That morning, when ye fainted, I knew that I would do anything to protect you, but here, in this time, you don't need my protection. I watched you work with your family; you give so much to those around you. You take care of people, but at the end of the day, who takes care of you? I know I am supposed to leave tomorrow, but I wanted to ask ye. What if I dinna go?"

He looked at Hannah, and she stood there, her eyes wide, her mouth open, tears streaming down her face. Graham felt panic rising. It was the moment. He had to convince her, or this would be their last night together.

"Hannah, we can work it out. I know ye have that job in the city. We both know I dinna care for the city, but I care very much for you. I would rather live in that loud, noisy city and have ye in my life than ne'er see ye again. Look through the rest of the binder. You will find my five-year plan and how I plan to support our family, should we have one. I'll not pressure ye, but I just wanted ye to know how I feel. I love you. I want to take care of you. I want to make ye happy. If ye will let me, I will spend every day of the rest of my life doing just that."

He looked at Hannah, waiting to see what she would say. Her expression was still unreadable. She just looked at him, shocked, surprised, crying.

"Hannah, please say something and put me out of my misery."

"Graham . . . I . . . I don't know what to say."

Graham felt his heart fall out of his chest. He gripped the table to support himself. She didn't want him. She didn't think he would fit into her life. He had lost her.

"No, Graham," she said. She walked over to him and took his hands. "Come with me. I have something to show you."

She led him upstairs to her bedroom. When she opened the door, he saw a room bathed in candlelight and flower petals leading to the bed.

It was Graham's turn to look at her like a codfish.

"What's all this?"

"Graham, I have something I wanted to say to you tonight, too."

She closed her eyes and took a deep breath.

"Tha goal agam art. Feuch gum fuirich thu còmhia rium gu bráth." *I love you, please stay here with me.*

Graham took her face in his hands. "Those were the sweetest Gaelic words I've ever heard." He pressed a gentle kiss to her lips. "Also the worst. We need to work on yer Gaelic, mo ghrádh, especially if yer choosing life with a highlander."

He held her close for a moment. "So, ye want me to stay?" He wanted to make sure he wasn't dreaming.

"Why do you think I've been throwing myself at you? I was trying to show you what you would be missing. I was trying to make it so you couldn't live without me."

"Hannah, dinna get me wrong, I have immensely appreciated yer enthusiasm in the past couple days. Ye fulfilled fantasies I dinna even know I had, but what I feel for ye is so much more than beddin' ye. Ye must know that by now. I have been trying to be a gentleman and show ye I could fit into your world. That I can be a partner to ye and contribute to a life together."

"Graham, I have never doubted that. You are a strong, capable man, in this time or any. And if we are being honest, I have loved you since that night by the fire when I sprained my ankle. That weekend with my sister throwing herself at you, my family drama and then me getting drunk, and spraining my ankle. You weren't scared off, and more than that, you were an unwavering support, and you have been ever since. You have filled in the gaps I have just learned to live with. You make my life better, and you make me happy."

She got a little choked up getting out the last words, and tears started streaming down her face again. Graham wrapped his arms around her and held her to his chest. He could feel her body crying against his. His own tears welling up in his eyes. He tried to blink them away, but they streamed down his face.

"Hush now mo ghrádh. Dinna fash."

Hannah looked up at him and smiled through tears.

"Why not? You're fashing, too."

Graham chuckled. "Aye, we are both being silly. Just think, we spent the past two days worried the other one was going to send us away, and here we are now." He pulled her back to his chest. This is where she belonged. She belonged in his arms.

"I mean, a witch did bring you through time to me. I think we should give it a go," she said, her voice muffled in his chest.

"Aye, I do believe yer right."

Hannah pushed herself away from him and looked around.

"And, Graham, did you really make a five-year plan?"

"Of course, there is even a PowerPoint presentation"

"How did you learn to do all that stuff?" she asked in amazement.

"Sam showed me some things, and I learned how to use YouTube. You can learn anything on there."

"But I thought you couldn't wait to get back to your own time? I was going to ask you to stay at Christmas, but I heard you talking in the barn about how you couldn't wait to go back to your own time and how much you hated it here."

"What?" His face struck with utter bewilderment. He had been taking steps to stay at that time.

"I did! I heard you. That's why I accepted the job that my dad ambushed me with. I was going to decline, but I went in and accepted it."

"That's why ye started actin' so funny after Christmas. I had spoken to yer father earlier that day about some plans for the land that would benefit both him and the orchard. He asked me to email him the plans. What ye heard was me trying to send a blasted email." He cupped her face in his hands.

"What?"

"Hannah, I have known I didn't want to leave for a long time, but since the first time I made you fall apart on my hand, I knew I would do anything in my power to make ye happy and never leave ye."

"I only accepted the job because I thought this was over, and I needed to get back to the real world. When my dad was in the hospital, we had a talk. The basic gist of it is, is that he wants me to be happy, and if I am happy here not being a lawyer, then I shouldn't do it. He gave me the farm, Graham. This is ours. He said we could do whatever we wanted with it."

"Hannah, at some point, I am going to tell ye about all the plans I shared with yer father and start our life, but right now, I would very much like to kiss you."

"Not if I kiss you first."

Her mouth found his like it was home. This time, she kissed him slowly. He relished in the slowness of the kiss, knowing this wasn't goodbye. This was a kiss to start building a life together with the woman he loved. He was overcome. It was still hard to believe that it was only the beginning. He pulled out of the kiss, looked at her, and tucked a loose strand of blonde hair behind her ear.

"You are mine, Hannah Glenn, now and always."

"And you are mine, highlander."

He kissed her deeply one more time, holding her close to him.

That night, he took her to bed, and they spent the night in each other's arms. They made love, and it felt like the first time. It felt like love. It always had been love, but there was no need to rush; they had each other and the future they would make their own.

THAT NEXT NIGHT when they were supposed to do the return spell, Hannah came downstairs, holding the bag that the witch at the ren faire had given them.

"What are ye goin' to do with that?" he asked suspiciously.

"I don't know. What do you think we should do with it?"

"I don't know, but I think we need to get rid of it. We can't accidentally send me back. Maybe we should burn it? Bury it? Maybe we don't do anything with it."

Hannah looked at it.

"It says we should open it on March 20th? So, maybe we open it?"

"I dinna feel right about this. I dinna trust witches."

"There's the stubborn superstitious Scotsman I love," she said to him with a smile. "I think we should, at least, open it."

Graham looked at her, shaking his head. He didn't want to be magically sent away in the same manner in which he was magically brought. That was a mistake he didn't want to correct, but Hannah had ripped it open. He looked at her, and he was trying to read her face. She looked confused.

"For the love of Christ, what is it?"

"It's not a spell," she said.

"What do you mean?"

"Well, she gave me a blend of herbs and an incantation and specific directions to bring you here. This is just an envelope with your name on it."

"What?"

"It is. Look." She pulled out a plain envelope with Graham MacNeil written on it.

"There is nothing else in there?"

"Nope, this is it. Should I open it?" Without waiting for an answer, she slid her finger under the seal and pulled out some papers. "Oh my god."

"What is it?"

She showed him a stack of official paperwork.

"It is your birth certificate, a paper of dual citizenship, a social security card. Graham, this is all you need to be a documented person. This means you can get a driver's license. This means we can get married, all those things. It means you officially belong here."

"What?" he asked, pulling the papers from her hand.

"See? It's all there."

Graham stared at the papers, dumbfounded. This was going to make life considerably easier for them. He would be able to work and provide for her. He would be able to marry her and spend the rest of his life making her happy.

"Who was that woman? Geez! I mean, I'm not going to complain or anything but wow. She wasn't messing around. And how did she know I wasn't ready to send your sorry ass back to the 1700s?"

"The same way she ken to bring me to ye. I think it's best not to ask such questions and just be glad that we get to spend the rest of our life together."

"Ya know what, I agree," she said, sliding her arms around his waist.

Graham continued to look at the papers. There were many things in life he couldn't explain, but this topped them all, and he wasn't about to ask questions. He set the papers on the counter and kissed the top of Hannah's head, breathing in her shampoo. He loved the way she smelled. He loved the way her soft body melted into his. He loved the fire in her eyes when she was all riled up. He loved the smolder in her eyes when they made love. He also loved that they had a lifetime stretched out before them for him to find more things that he loved about her. He had a notion he would never stop finding things to love about Hannah Glenn.

This was just the beginning.

EPILOGUE

 wo Years Later

HANNAH LOOKED out the window as she poured her coffee, watching her handsome highlander chop wood. It still made her melt, but some things had changed. The yard, which had once been a pristine landscaped retreat for a rich family of city dwellers, was turned into a home, not only a home but a family farm.

She looked over the field that housed chickens, sheep, and a few cows—the cute, fluffy highland cows, of course—all filling her with peace.

Graham had helped Sam start a petting zoo for the orchard. He cared for the animals there and the ones they had. He helped Sam run some of the new features of the orchard, which had succeeded in making the orchard a tourist destination. Graham also ran the farm like a living museum. He lived and worked the farm like he did back in Scotland, kilt and all. He lived a life that used all his skills to provide for them, and Hannah would never grow tired of her highlander chopping wood out there in a kilt.

Hannah was writing her next book. She had published her first book to unexpected success. She was offered a deal for two more books. She felt so happy to be living her life. They had already had their happy ending when they got married on the fall equinox, one year to the day that they both woke up to find their lives forever altered. They wanted to get married then, so the miracle matchmaking witch who brought them together could be in attendance. She was happy to be there. Graham didn't shake her once. He did give her a big bear hug, picking her up off the ground. It was a wonderful day.

The door in the kitchen opened, and Hannah looked over to find Graham walking in, looking very much like he did the first day they met. Same kilt and coat, big boots, and his red hair tied back. He looked like a relic from the past in the hottest way possible.

"Mo ghrádh, I do believe ye are to be cutting back on caffeine," he said. He walked over to Hannah and put his hand on her belly. He kissed her. Then he bent down and kissed her belly. "Good morning, mo leanbh."

"This is my first cup. The doctor said I could have one cup."

Hannah was just starting to show, with their first baby.

"I ken, and I trust ye with yer own body. I'm just so excited for our bairn to come."

"Well, I gotta get this book written before he comes."

"Or she—I think I might like a wee lass. We can raise her to be as strong and stubborn as her mother," he said. He smacked Hannah's ass and turned to pour himself a cup of coffee. "I have a field trip coming at 10:30. After that, I am done for the day. Whenever ye are ready for break, I have a surprise for ye in the barn."

"Okay, I'll be out. I'm hoping to knock out a couple chapters today." She grabbed a muffin and her coffee and gave Graham a kiss before heading to her office.

The room that used to be her father's masculine office, with dark wood and sleek surfaces, had become her office, which was filled with a cozy reading nook and fuzzy blankets and pillows. The bookshelves that once housed law and old leather-bound books, had been replaced by romance novels, floor to ceiling. Teacups and piles of unkempt papers with research and manuscripts in the process of being edited scattered her desk.

Her dad had given her this farmhouse, and they had made some changes. They had truly made this house a home, and soon, a baby would arrive—a bairn, as they'd say. Graham's Gaelic was something Hannah found herself using more often as time went on.

After the field trip ended and all the kids piled back onto the big yellow bus. Hannah headed out to the barn to see Graham's surprise. He covered her eyes and led her to the back office in the barn. He removed his hands, revealing a beautifully carved cradle.

"I made this for the bairn. I ken we have a room with a beautiful crib, and all the things yer mother bought, but I thought we might keep this in our room so we can be close to the bairn as it sleeps."

"It's beautiful, Graham. You are going to be an amazing father."

"I will spend my life trying to be. Of that, I am certain. I am also certain you will be a good mother. I love you, Hannah Glenn."

Her decision to keep her own name was something Graham had scoffed at when she had first brought it up, but in the end, what he loved most about Hannah was her strength.

The way they got together was magical and unconventional, and their lifestyle was, too. They found purpose and passion in their daily lives, but that didn't hold a candle to the passion they got to share at night with each other. Hannah was living a life she once didn't even allow herself to dream of, all because of a love spell that brought her true love.

And, in the end, the life they built together was better than any happily ever after she could dream up for one of her books.

AFTERWORD

Hello Readers,

I hope you enjoyed Hannah and Graham's love story. Did you maybe wonder what would have happened if Hannah went back to the past? Well, I wondered the same thing. If you would like to find out you can sign up for my newsletter and I will send you a bonus story about how Hannah and Graham would have faired in the past.

Newletter

Also be sure to check for *Spotlight on Poppy* which will be coming in the spring 2023.

Poppy gets a love spell of her own and there is a little confusion when a stranger comes to town. Find out how this spell will work to help Poppy find love.

ACKNOWLEDGMENTS

I have so many people to thank for this book. It has been a labor of love and a long time coming. It has been a dream of mine ever since I was a child to write a book, and I did it. It is a massive sense of accomplishment, but I know I could not have done it without the help of many others.

Will, my heart, my alpha reader, my sounding board, my partner in this crazy thing we call life. Thank you for all of your unending support, for all the dinners your brought to my desk while I was writing, for all of the writer's block you talked me through, for all the slack you pick up when I had to go into my writer's hidey hole. The love and appreciation I feel for you is beyond words.

Fat Girls in Fiction community, you guys are the best. You keep me inspired and give me a reason to keep moving on days when the imposter syndrome sets in hard. I pour so much into this community because I believe all people in fat bodies are deserving of love and achieving their wildest dreams.

Olivia Dade, I'm not sure any of this would have been possible with out her books. She showed me what was possible. *Spoiler Alert* was the first time I ever saw an unapologetic fat person getting love and a happy ending. This is why representation is so important, you can need something deep in your soul but not be able to put words to it because you're not even sure it exists. *Spoiler Alert* opened my eyes to this representation, it has been the most healing journey I have ever taken. Her books did for me what years of therapy could never do. Now I will write my own stories about fat women finally getting the happy endings they deserve, because we are worth it. Thank you for sharing your stories and beginning a healing journey that has been profound and life changing.

Leni Kauffman, this cover is absolute perfection. It brought my characters to life is such a beautiful and loving way. It is a rare artist who can find the beauty in fat bodies but their covers always deliver. Perfection. Absolute perfection.

My team, my editor, Samantha at Misseloquentedits, thank you for helping to make my writing better. My fabulous beta readers, thank you for making my story the best it could be.

And I also want to thank my readers. Yes, you, thank you. Thank you for taking a chance on Hannah and Graham. I hope I did not disappont and you will be back for more stories with a little bit of magic and a whole lot of heart.

ABOUT THE AUTHOR

Mary Warren lives in Illinois with her family. When she's not writing stories of fat women, she's reading them and advocating for better fat representation. Mary founded Fat Girls in Fiction, pointing out positive fat representation for women, femmes, and non-binary people in books. This project became a community and is something she is immensely proud of and happy to be working on.

Lightning Source UK Ltd.
Milton Keynes UK
UKHW011829040123
414830UK00006B/561